Book three in the Hal Junior series

www.haljunior.com

Published by Bowman Press

Internal illustrations by Simon Haynes

ISBN 978-1-877034-36-7 (Ebook)
ISBN 978-1-877034-24-4 (Paperback)

National Library of Australia Cataloguing-in-Publication entry
Author: Haynes, Simon, 1967-
Title: The Gyris Mission / Simon Haynes.
ISBN: 9781877034244 (pbk.)
Series: Haynes, Simon, 1967- Hal Junior ; 3.
Target Audience: For primary school age.
Subjects: Science fiction--Juvenile fiction.
Dewey Number: A823.4

Simon Haynes

Bowman Press

The Hal Junior Series:

The Secret Signal
The Missing Case
The Gyris Mission
The Comet Caper

Simon Haynes also writes the
Hal Spacejock series for teens & adults

... AND the
Harriet Walsh series for teens & adults.

www.spacejock.com.au

Dedicated to keen readers everywhere

Hal Junior, accepting a bet,
cooked lunch on a ship's exhaust jet.
His bacon burned, smoking,
The eggs had no yolk in,
And his toast has not been found yet!

— 1 —

My, robot

It was just before dawn, and a large group of Peace Force officers were gathered in the briefing room. They were travelling aboard the Almara, an elderly Battlecruiser which had been disguised as a transport ship. Their mission was simple: take down a gang of pirates who were terrorizing the Lamira system.

The mess doors opened, and a hush fell over the crowd. Standing in the doorway was the most famous, the most impressive and the most capable officer of them all: Captain Hal Spacejock of the Intergalactic Peace Force!

'Morning all,' said Spacejock. 'What's going on here, then?'

Nobody spoke, until a huge bull of a man with a thick neck timidly raised his hand. 'Please sir, we need a battle plan.'

'You want a plan? I'll give you a plan!' Spacejock drew himself up to his full height. 'We're going to charge straight in and clean out those dastardly pirates!'

The mess hall erupted with cheers, and –

'Good morning, Hal Junior. And how are we this fine day?'

Hal opened one eye and saw a robot smiling down at him. It had a wrinkly bronze face and bright yellow eyes, and it looked way too cheerful for such an early hour. The robot was Clunk, Hal's new tutor, and it took its job very seriously. 'How can it be morning?' demanded Hal. 'It's still dark.'

'I thought you'd like an early start. You know what day it is, don't you?'

Hal felt a sudden thrill. Of course he did. 'The day of the camping trip. It's finally here?' He leapt out of bed and grabbed the nearest pile of clothes, getting dressed in such a hurry he put both arms down the same sleeve, pulled on odd socks and jammed his shoes on the wrong feet. 'Is the gear ready? I don't want to forget anything.'

'Equipment status a-okay,' said Clunk. 'I spent all night packing and re-packing our things, from tents to sleeping bags to emergency food rations.'

'Wait a minute. What do you mean 'our' things? This is a school trip.'

Clunk looked surprised. 'I thought you knew? I'm coming as well.'

Hal groaned. Clunk was all right, as far as robots went, but who wanted to take their tutor on holidays?

'Apart from the packing, I also created some really interesting maths homework. There's nothing better than mental arithmetic when you're sitting around a campfire.'

Hal groaned even louder.

'Are you all right?' asked Clunk. 'Do you have stomach ache? Should I take you to the sickbay?'

'No, I'm fine,' said Hal, trying not to laugh at Clunk's expression. Robots didn't get sick, and illness in humans always worried them. 'You're not really coming to Gyris, are you?'

'Of course. Now, do you want to check the bags?'

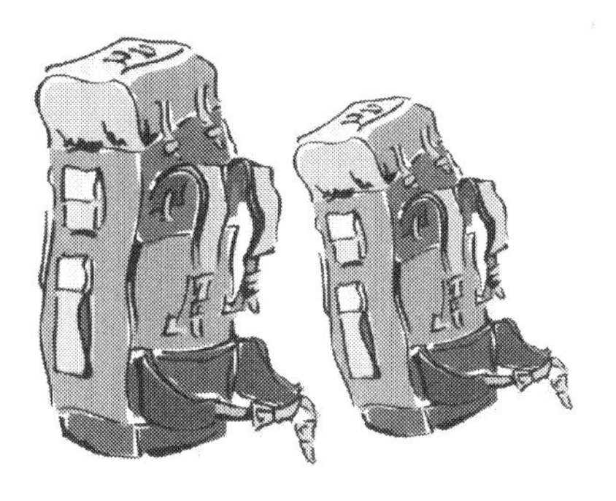

Hal followed Clunk to the doorway, where there were two bulging rucksacks. Clunk opened the bigger one and displayed a roll of clear plastic and a bundle of metal poles. 'They didn't give me a tent, so I made my own.'

'What else do you have?'

'I brought all your winter clothing.'

'Clunk, it's summer down there.'

'It might be cold at night.'

'What if it's really hot?'

'That's all right, because I have all your summer clothing too. And three pairs of pyjamas, and that dressing gown you like. You know, the one with the teddy bear on the side.'

Hal stared at him in horror. 'I used to wear that when I was five. You didn't really pack it, did you?'

'Of course. It's warm and cosy.'

'You have to get rid of it. Take it out of right now, or I'll never speak to you again.'

'Don't worry, you can always use it as a pillow.'

Hal resolved to throw it out the first chance he got. 'What else did you bring? A big packet of nappies? Baby food?'

'Of course not. There's a solar-powered charger, in case my batteries need topping up, and I have all your old schoolwork. I thought we could go over your completed assignments and see where you went wrong. For example, there was one on heavy metals which . . .'

Hal started to groan, then turned it into a cough.

'That's it,' said Clunk. 'We're off to the sickbay right now.'

'Clunk, I'm fine. It was just a bit of dust.'

The robot looked at him suspiciously, and Hal put on his most innocent expression. 'Very well, but if you so much as sniff I'm taking you for a full medical.'

'If you do, I'll miss the camping trip.'

'If you're unwell, the camping trip is out of the question.'

'For the last time, I am not sick!'

'There's no need to take that tone with me. Now, are you feeling well enough for a proper breakfast or would you prefer dry bread and a glass of water?'

Hal groaned.

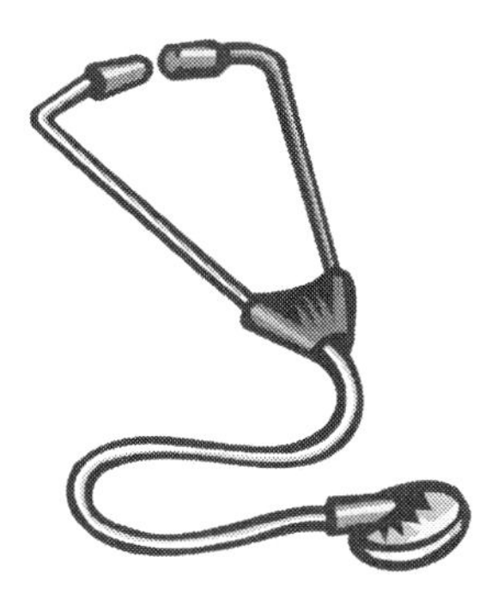

In the sickbay, the doctor got Hal to walk through the med scanner before giving them her diagnosis: all clear. Clunk frowned, and got her to put Hal through the big machine again, and after the third time the doctor struggled to keep her temper. 'I'm telling you, there is nothing wrong with this child,' she said, annoyed. 'He's fitter than I am.'

'But he keeps groaning,' protested Clunk. 'There was even . . . a cough.'

The doctor frowned at Hal over her glasses. 'Are you trying to get a sick note? Avoid school?'

'No chance,' said Hal. 'I'm going camping.'

'Well, have a nice time.' The doctor rang a little bell. 'Next patient, please.'

Clunk was silent as they left the sickbay. He didn't like being wrong, and he was convinced the doctor's machine hadn't analysed Hal properly. 'I still believe she rushed your DNA test.'

'Clunk, she's a doctor. Even if you don't believe me, you have to believe her. I am not sick.'

The robot sighed noisily.

'Was that an air leak?' asked Hal mischievously. 'Should I take you to the repair centre for a checkup?'

Clunk smiled apologetically. 'I'm sorry, Hal. I take my job very seriously.'

'I take breakfast seriously, and I'm missing it.'

— 2 —

Departure

'Would all students please report to passenger lounge two. I repeat, would all students please report to passenger lounge two without delay.' There was a pause. 'That means you, Hal Junior.'

Hal pushed his plate back and jumped up. 'Come on, Clunk. We're off.'

'You haven't finished your breakfast.'

'That's all right, you can have it.'

Clunk started to object, but Hal was already in the corridor. When Hal looked back, he saw Clunk struggling to follow with the heavy rucksacks.

Hal ran through the Space Station's corridors at top speed, taking his favourite shortcuts and the fastest elevators. Each time he stepped out of a lift he pressed the top and bottom buttons, sending it to the Station's highest and lowest levels. With a bit of luck, Clunk would still be waiting for a lift when the passenger ship left the space station.

Hal finally arrived at the passenger lounge, where he found the rest of his class sitting on benches. Teacher was there, and the little red robot was darting around as he tried to keep an electronic eye on the children. There were also three parents, volunteers who were coming along to help out on the camping trip.

'Hal, over here. I saved you a seat!'

Hal saw his best friend Stephen 'Stinky' Binn waving like mad, and he hurried over to sit next to him.

'Where have you been?' demanded Stinky. 'We're leaving any second.'

'Clunk took me to the sickbay,' explained Hal.

'More groaning, huh? I warned you about that.'

'I coughed, too.'

'You're lucky he didn't take you to intensive care.'

Hal saw Clunk in the doorway, and he ducked his head. 'Don't tell him I'm here.'

Stinky watched the robot's progress, giving Hal a running commentary. 'He's asking Teacher about you. Now Teacher's looking around. Oh, he's seen you. Now they're both coming over.'

Hal sat up. 'Hi Teacher. Are we leaving now?'

'Hal Junior, why is your tutor here?'

Hal couldn't answer many of Teacher's questions,

but he knew the answer to this one. 'Clunk is here to teach me.'

Teacher frowned. 'I meant here, here. Present in this room, and carrying two rucksacks. Why?'

'He offered to carry them. They're heavy.'

'Yes, but why is he here?'

'Er, to teach me?'

'Here, here, here!' said Teacher, jabbing his finger at the floor to emphasise each word.

'You mean here?' said Hal.

'Here!'

'He's coming with us.'

'Thank you, that's what I thought.' Teacher turned to Clunk. 'I'm afraid there's been a misunderstanding. You cannot go on this trip.'

Clunk stared. 'But . . . I have to look after Hal.'

'Hal Junior will be supervised, just like the other students.'

'I already packed a bag, and a battery charger, and a big umbrella to keep the rain off. I even made my own tent.'

Teacher shook his head. 'The students must learn to cope on their own. They're travelling without robots.'

'So how come you're going?' demanded Clunk.

'I'm not. I'm staying here.'

Hal stared. No tutor and no Teacher? This was going to be the best trip ever!

'But Hal's homework . . .' began Clunk.

'There will be no homework.'

'His revision . . .'

'No revision.'

By now Hal was grinning from ear to ear.

Clunk's shoulders slumped, and his expression was downcast. 'I'm not needed?'

'Oh, you're very much needed,' said Teacher. 'Next week Hal Junior will need double homework to catch up.'

'Get set, people. We're moving out in five!'

Captain Spacejock's assault team checked their weapons, inspecting battery levels and charge leads. Around them, the docking bay was piled high with equipment, and the boarding tunnel gaped like a giant mouth. Any moment now they'd board the landing craft, and –

'Teacher, Hal Junior keeps pushing me!'

Hal blinked, and the daydream faded. He'd just been reloading a really cool blast rifle, and in the process his elbow had rammed someone in the ribs.

Teacher rolled towards him, every eye on his electronic face focused on Hal. 'Hal Junior, if you cause any more trouble you'll stay behind. Is that clear?'

Hal nodded and crossed his arms. The class was still waiting in the passenger lounge next to the Space Station's docking bay. There were three rows of bench seats, but they weren't big enough for two dozen active children, and complaints came thick and fast. Teacher sped from one incident to the next, trying to maintain order, but eventually the little robot snapped. He screeched to a halt at the front of the room and turned his voice to maximum volume.

'Listen to me!' he roared, shaking the walls with the sound of his voice.

Everyone froze, and there was instant silence.

'I know you've been looking forward to this camping trip for weeks, but the next person to make a fuss will stay right here on the Space Station with me. Instead of camping, you'll be studying!'

Hal realised Teacher was looking at him, and he swallowed nervously. He'd already been banned from the trip once, after the practice campfire incident*, and getting excluded a second time would be unbearable.

'One raised voice, one complaint, one incident, and I won't hesitate to ban any of you from the trip. Is that clear?'

The entire class spoke as one. 'Yes, Teacher!'

'Thank you. Now sit tight and be patient. I'm sure the transport will be ready soon.'

Hal glanced at his big silver space watch. They were supposed to have left at nine, and it was already eleven o'clock. First the ship had been late, and then there'd been refuelling problems, and now they were just waiting around. Morning snacks, meant to be eaten later, had been finished off long ago, and all their luggage had already gone aboard so they had nothing to keep them busy.

'I have an exciting idea,' said Teacher brightly. 'Who'd like to answer a few math questions?'

Hal groaned, then looked around quickly in case Clunk had heard him. Fortunately the robot wasn't there.

Teacher projected the first sums on the wall, and Stinky was just revealing the answers when the doors opened with a *whisshhh.*

A woman in a grey flightsuit looked in. 'Get set, people. We're moving out in five!'

---

* *Hal Junior: The Missing Case*

— 3 —

Boarding

The next few minutes passed in a blur. One moment they were saying goodbye to Teacher, and the next they were escorted out of the lounge by the parents who were supervising the trip. Hal was secretly glad his own parents weren't going. His dad was in charge of the Space Station's air filters, and he was too busy to take a week off. As for Hal's mum, she was the Station's chief scientist, and she couldn't possibly spare a week away from the laboratory.

Hal didn't mind at all. No parents meant more freedom!

The class trooped along the boarding tunnel and navigated the airlock at the far end. They had to go through in batches, because the airlock wasn't big enough for everyone. On the other side, an official from the space station showed them through a pair of doors. Inside, there was a lounge set up like a small cinema: thick carpeting, comfortable chairs arranged in rows, and a big screen at the front. Hal's heart sank as he saw the heavy curtains along both sides. He'd expected a good view of the stars, but it looked like they were going to get movies all the way to Gyris. Then he had a horrible thought . . . what if Teacher had chosen a bunch of educational documentaries as their 'entertainment'?

Hal came up with a plan. If they were forced to watch documentaries, he and Stinky would ask to go to the toilet. Once on their own, they'd explore the whole ship. If anyone from the crew spotted them, he'd use the old 'sorry, we got lost' excuse. It was amazing how often that worked, almost as though adults expected kids to get lost all the time.

Hal turned to explain his plan to Stinky, but at that moment the lights went out and the screen came alive.

'Welcome aboard the Antigone, a state-of-the-art passenger transport with every known comfort.' The screen displayed a series of animations, showing the spaceship from the outside, before zooming in on the passenger lounge. 'In the unlikely event of an emergency, please make your way to the escape pods.' Arrows showed the exit route, taking the elevator down to an area with a dozen red dots. The flashing dots separated from the ship and flew into space. 'Each pod carries four people, and contains two weeks' worth of food and water. An emergency beacon will help rescue ships locate and retrieve each pod.'

Hal watched the video with interest. So, if they were attacked by a fleet of space pirates, and the Antigone was blown to smithereens, he could use one of those cool pods to get away. Then he could get hold of some ships, lead a daring raid on the pilot base to take over all their ships, and then, before you knew it, he'd rule the galaxy.

'For your comfort,' continued the video, 'toilets are located just outside the passenger lounge. Please note that all other parts of the vessel are off-limits.'

Hal's eyes narrowed. It was going to be pretty hard to get 'lost' when the toilets were that close, but he'd come up with some excuse. Maybe he could tell them he was looking for a glass of water!

'Refreshments are served automatically, via the dispenser in your armrest. Each passenger will be issued with a sterilised feeding tube after departure. Alcoholic beverages will not be served to minors.'

Hal lifted the lid on his armrest and looked inside. There was a touch screen and a silver connector with a hole in the middle. He tried the screen but it beeped and displayed a message:

Status: Inactive. Refreshments only available in flight.

'And now, please settle back for this screening of 'Attack the Summit!', a popular documentary on mountain climbing.'

Hal groaned. Popular was right . . . Teacher showed the same film every week. It had been pretty cool the first time Hal saw it, and it was still interesting the second time around, but after half a dozen showings he was desperate for a different ending. An avalanche, for example, or a wild Yeti. But no, every time it was the same.

Before the documentary started, the words 'NEWS FLASH' appeared, and the screen showed a smartly-dressed lady with glasses. 'This message is for all ships landing on planet Gyris. Two criminals are on the run after holding up a bank. The fugitives stole a low-orbital flyer to make their escape, and they're considered armed and dangerous.'

The screen changed to show grainy footage of two people in balaclavas. They were carrying a couple of heavy boxes, and they kicked open the bank doors before running out of view.

'Members of the public are warned to keep clear. Do not approach these vicious criminals, and please call the Peace Force if you have any information. Anyone helping these fugitives escape justice will be locked up right alongside them.'

Hal glanced at Stinky. 'I wonder if there's a reward?'

'Don't even think about it.'

At that moment the lights went out, and the screen glowed in the darkness. 'Attack the Summit' was beginning. Hal nudged Stinky, then nodded towards the exit. His friend frowned and shook his head, but Hal wasn't taking no for an answer. They got up and pushed their way along the row, treading on feet and stumbling over stray shins. A minor commotion followed them across the room, and one of the parents turned to see what was happening. Hal ducked, pulling Stinky down with him, and they peered between the seats until the adult turned away.

They reached the door, and as the dramatic title

music washed over the audience, Hal operated the controls and slipped through. Stinky followed, and the door closed with a whish!

'What are you playing at?' demanded Stinky. 'We'll miss the movie!'

Hal made a rude noise. 'I'll never miss that movie again. For my entire life. Ever.'

'Teacher does play it a lot,' admitted his friend.

'A lot! I could climb that stupid mountain blindfolded.'

Stinky laughed. 'So what's the plan?'

'We're aboard a spaceship, right?'

'Yes, I kind of knew that.'

'We're going to explore.'

'But Hal . . . we could get into trouble! Teacher might –'

'Teacher isn't here, is he?' Hal jabbed his finger at the door. 'Those parents will believe any excuse we feed them. Now stop yabbering and start exploring.'

— 4 —

Exploring

Hal scanned the signs on the wall outside the lounge. Opposite there were two doors with toilet symbols. To his right was the airlock they'd used to board the ship. To his left . . . well, that was the door which interested Hal the most. It had a sign reading 'No Admittance', and there was a keypad at shoulder height. The display on the keypad was broken, and half the numbers had worn away. There were wires hanging out of the keypad, and Hal eyed them in concern. 'Do you think it's working?'

'Someone bypassed it,' said Stinky. 'That's an RT-3D, the one with the defective security chip.'

Hal smiled to himself. Stinky lived and breathed electronics, and half the time he suspected his friend was a robot in disguise. 'Can you open it?'

'Sure. Purple wire crossed with orange. Watch.'

Hal's dad often told him how dangerous electricity could be, warning him never to play with bare wires. However, Stinky had already completed two certificates in electronics, and he knew what he was doing. At least, Hal hoped he did. 'Will it go bang?'

'Of course not. These are data wires, not electrical.' Stinky touched the wires together, and the door slid open. Beyond was a short corridor with three more doors: elevator, flight deck and galley.

Hal loved to study spaceship diagrams in his spare time, and he knew the galley was where food was prepared. He also knew he wasn't going to waste exploring time looking at kitchen equipment. That left the flight deck and the elevator. Now, exploring the flight deck would be cool, but there was one tiny problem: that's where the crew of highly-trained pilots would be.

So, the only door they could use was the elevator. Hal hesitated for a moment, his finger over the call button. Going further into the ship was bound to lead to trouble, and they could still return to the lounge. Then he smiled. They were already on their way to Gyris. Nobody could send him home again.

He pressed the button, and the doors opened slowly. The lift was big enough for eight or ten people, and the walls were dented and battered. There was a security camera in one corner of the roof, but it was dangling by the cord and the lens was missing.

Hal inspected the control panel, which had three buttons. He was on the upper deck now, and the others read 'Middle Deck' and 'Lower Deck'. None of them offered any clues as to what he might find on each level, but Hal didn't mind. Anything was better than watching Teacher's documentaries!

He pressed the button for the Middle Deck, and the lift started to move. As it squeaked and groaned its way to the next level, Hal checked his watch. The documentary ran for about thirty minutes, and he'd left the lounge five minutes ago. That left . . . lots of minutes to explore.

30 - 5 = LOTS!

The doors opened and Hal peeked out. He saw a long corridor with several doors on either side, and a dirty yellow carpet on the floor. It wasn't very promising, and he was about to press the third button when he noticed a sign on one of the doors: Escape pods. 'Hey, these were in the safety video.'

‘Indeed,’ said Stinky. ‘Safety pods are essential aboard space ships. Only the most careless pilot would travel without one.’

‘Captain Spacejock doesn’t use a sissy escape pod.’

Stinky rolled his eyes. Hal’s fixation with Captain Spacejock was a running joke in class. ‘I suppose your precious captain can breath without air?’

‘Of course. He’s generally modified.’

Stinky looked puzzled. ‘He’s what?’

‘He had his trousers altered,’ explained Hal. ‘You know, like Teacher was telling us.’

Hal’s explanation only had Stinky more confused. ‘How does altering your trousers help you breath in space?’

‘They’re not just any trousers. Captain Spacejock has special jeans.’

Stinky started to laugh, and before long he was gasping for breath, tears in his eyes. ‘It’s not ’generally modified’,’ he said, when he’d got his breath back. ‘It’s genetically modified! Genes, not jeans.’

‘That’s what I said,’ snapped Hal, aggrieved.

‘Okay, okay,’ said Stinky. ‘There’s no need to get . . . shirty.’ He snorted at the joke, and then he was laughing again, leaning against the wall for support.

Hal abandoned his friend and strode towards the escape pod doors. In the training video the pods had shot about like mini space fighters, and Hal figured it would be cool to see one up close. The sign said 'pods 1-6', while the door on the opposite side had 'pods 7-12'. Each door had a control panel with a single button, and Hal pressed one and waited.

Nothing happened.

'Maybe you have the wrong jeans on,' called Stinky, and he fell about laughing again.

Scowling, Hal thumped the button. The door remained closed, so he turned to the opposite side and pressed that button instead.

Whoosh!

This door opened immediately, revealing a semi-circular room with half a dozen silver doors in the opposite wall. They were evenly-spaced, and each had a status panel alongside. Five of the panels glowed green, while the last was red. Hal strode to the nearest door and studied the panel. There were buttons marked 'open' and 'close', and there was a red safety cap covering a third button marked 'launch'. The status display said 'System Okay' in bright green letters.

Hal hesitated, then pressed the Open button. The door slid up with a Whissh!, and he looked down into the pod. The walls were padded, and there was a bench seat running all the way around. In the middle was a round console, and four heavy-duty harnesses dangled from the ceiling. It looked comfortable and cosy, and Hal almost wished there could be an emergency so they could use the pods to fly through space. Nothing dangerous, just a minor problem like a killer asteroid or heavily-armed space aliens.

'Hal, what are you doing?' hissed Stinky, from the safety of the doorway. He'd stopped laughing, and was now looking worried. 'You can't play with this stuff. It's dangerous.'

Hal decided to punish his friend for laughing at him, and before Stinky could intervene he'd stepped down into the pod. Hal sat on the chair and fitted the harness, tightening the straps until he could barely move. The central console was just out of reach, but he could still read some of the controls: 'Open', 'close' and 'launch' buttons, along with several others labelled 'recycle', 'gravity' and 'boosters'.

Stinky's face appeared in the doorway. 'Hal, come out of there at once!'

'No, I think I'll take it for a spin,' said Hal. 'That'd be fun.'

'Hal! I'll tell!'

Hal glanced at his watch, then stared. Twenty minutes gone already! That only left them . . . several minutes to explore the rest of the ship.

30 - 20 = SEVERAL!

He undid the straps and climbed out of the pod, pausing only to press the 'Close' button.

'Let's go back now,' said Stinky. All traces of laughter were gone, and he looked worried.

'Nonsense. There's more to see.'

'But –'

Hal walked away. He was still smarting from Stinky's laughter, and he was enjoying getting his own back on his friend. Back in the corridor, he turned away from the lift and hurried along the mustard-yellow carpet. The roar of the engines got louder, and the doors he passed were labelled 'Starboard access' and 'Main power bus'. Finally, at the rear, there was a big metal door stamped 'Engine Bay'. There was also a warning sign underneath: 'Very Dangerous! No admittance without safety clothing.'

Hal was keen to explore, but he wasn't completely stupid. There were plenty of places aboard Space Station Oberon where you needed hazard suits, and he knew to stay well clear of them. That just left the lower deck to explore.

— 5 —

Crackle

The lower deck was more like Hal's idea of a genuine spaceship, with dim lighting and stark metal walls. The roof was low, and dusty wires and cables ran along channels under the floor.

Crackle-zzit! Crackle-zzzziit!

Flickering sparks bathed the corridor in harsh blue light, and Hal noticed a strong electrical smell.

'This doesn't look very safe,' remarked Stinky.

Hal gestured impatiently. 'It's a spaceship. It's not supposed to be safe.'

Crackle-zziit!

'Let's go back to the lounge,' said Stinky. 'Please, Hal. They'll notice we're missing.'

'I'm not going back until we've explored the whole ship.'

'But Hal!'

Hal ignored his friend and strode along the

corridor. He told himself it couldn't be that dangerous, or they wouldn't let people walk around down here. Then he remembered the 'No Admittance' sign on the upper deck, and swallowed. They didn't let people walk around down here. He and Stinky were trespassing.

Crackle-zziittt!

A blue flash illuminated a grubby sign on the wall. Hal brushed dirt off the sign, which said 'Maintenance'. He touched the controls and the door grated open. Inside, there was a status panel, the screen rolling and flickering like Teacher's face when he was trying to read one of Hal's essays. Hal tapped the screen, and it sat still long enough for him to read the display:

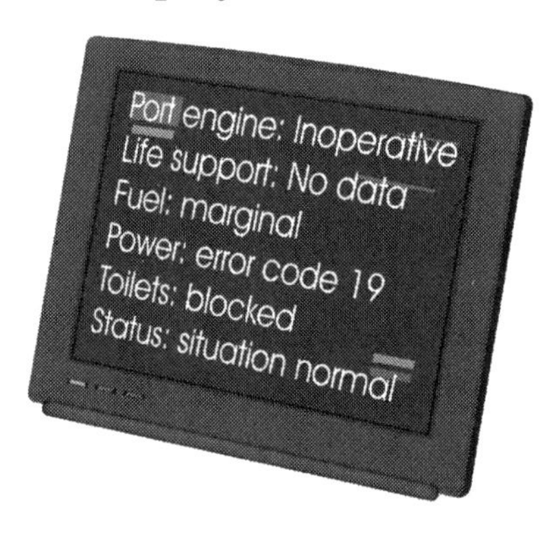

Hal grabbed his friend and dragged him to the maintenance alcove, and they both studied the display. From the look of all the warning messages, the ship was seconds from a major meltdown.

'This looks serious,' said Stinky.

'Too right. We have to warn someone.'

'I bet they already know,' said Stinky. 'The pilots will have the same display in the flight deck.'

'Maybe they haven't seen the warnings.' Hal had a thought, and he gripped Stinky's arm. 'Maybe they've fainted! Maybe aliens have captured them! Maybe we'll have to fly the ship to Gyris and land it!'

'Maybe you should give your imagination a holiday,' said Stinky drily.

'Let's go and tell the pilots about the error messages. They might let us sit in the flight deck.'

For once, Stinky didn't object, and the two boys took the lift to the upper deck. When the doors opened they hurried to the flight deck entrance, where they saw a sign written in big red letters:

Underneath, in thick blue marker, someone had written This Means You!

Hal was just reaching for the controls when Stinky stopped him. 'What?'

'Hal, we can't. We'll have to tell them we went to the lower deck.'

Hal thought for a moment. 'We'll say we got lost. All these passages look the same.'

'They know we live on a Space Station.'

Stinky had a point. The Space Station had five sections, each filled with endless lifts and corridors. If the boys could navigate something that complex, nobody would believe they could get lost aboard a tiny passenger ship. 'All right. We'll tell them we heard that buzz-crackle noise.'

'What, two decks up?'

'We have very good hearing.'

'It would have to be supersonic,' muttered Stinky.

'What was that?'

'Nothing.'

Hal took a deep breath and used the controls. The doors parted with a loud Whish!, and the two boys peered in. They saw a flight console covered in instruments, a big screen covered in charts and figures, two big pilot chairs and . . . no pilots.

'It's aliens!' breathed Hal. 'They've captured the crew!'

— 6 —

Asleep at the wheel

Bzzzz-glglglgl! Bzzzz-glglglgl!

Hal's eyes were as round as an airlock door. The weird sounds were coming from the back of the flightdeck, where a huddled mass was slumped against the wall.

Bzzzz-glglglgl!

Was it an alien monster, telling them to put their hands up? Was it a deadly sound weapon that would scramble their brains?

'Oh look, it's the pilot,' said Stinky, peering into the darkness. 'He's fast asleep.'

That awful noise was the pilot's snoring? Hal couldn't believe it. So much for alien invasions and sound weapons.

'We'd better wake him,' whispered Stinky. 'Nobody's flying the ship.'

‘Somebody is.’ Hal nodded towards the big screen, which had the words ’Autopilot Active’ in the corner.

‘What about all the error messages we saw on the lower deck?’

Hal hadn’t forgotten about them, but he didn’t want to wake the pilot. First, because the flight deck was calm and peaceful, as though everything were under control. And second, because there were two empty pilot chairs and two sets of controls just begging to be used. ‘I’m captain,’ muttered Hal out the corner of his mouth. ‘You’re my second in command.’

Stinky frowned. ‘What are you planning now?’

‘Let’s pretend the pilot really was kidnapped. Let’s pretend we have to fly the ship.’

‘Let’s not,’ said Stinky quickly.

But Hal wasn’t listening. He crossed the flight deck in three strides and turned the pilot’s chair to the side.

‘You can’t!’ hissed Stinky. ‘You mustn’t!’

‘Watch me,’ muttered Hal, and he sat down at the controls. His eyes shone as he scanned the status displays, lights and toggle switches, and there was a huge grin on his face when he spotted the flight controls. There was a joystick with a big red button on top, and two sliding throttles to control the engines. Excellent!

Stinky crept closer. He wasn't as bold as Hal, but he was just as interested in spaceships, and the chance to sit at the controls was too tempting. In a flash he was sitting in the second chair.

'Right,' said Hal. 'Let's explore the galaxy.'

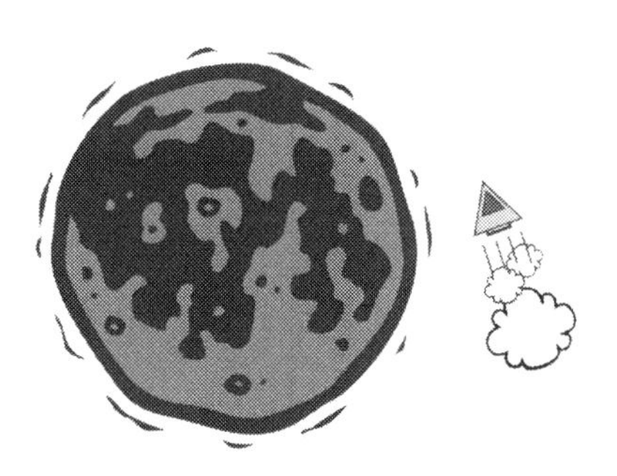

Hal and Stinky spent ten glorious minutes pretending to fly the passenger ship. They roamed all over the galaxy, with Stinky capturing alien planets and battlecruisers, while Hal claimed two dozen worlds for Queen Alexandra of Gyris. They were having so much fun it was a pity it had to end, but they realised they had to get back to the passenger lounge before the documentary ended.

'If they stick another film on I'm coming right back,' whispered Hal.

Stinky nodded, his eyes shining.

The pilot was still snoring behind them, lost to the world, and Hal hoped he stayed that way for the entire trip. Imagine if they could sit in the flight deck while the ship approached Gyris! And if the pilot slept through the whole thing, they could maybe even watch the landing. What a start to their camping trip!

The boys turned their chairs away from the controls and prepared to step down. Hal put a hand on the console to steady himself, and his fingers brushed a row of switches.

'Autopilot disabled,' said a calm female voice. *'You have manual control.'*

Hal froze, then slowly turned to look at the screen. It no longer said 'Autopilot Active' in the corner, and the stars weren't nice and still either . . . in fact, they were moving across the big screen. The ship was turning, and nobody was at the controls. If they kept this up they might end up back at the Orbiter, or lost in space!

Stinky gulped, and both boys stared at the console in horror. The pilot would know how to fix things, but if they woke him up they'd have to explain what they'd been doing in the flight deck. On the other hand, if they tried to activate the autopilot themselves, they could make things a whole lot worse.

Then Hal remembered something. He'd once toured a spaceship with the rest of his class, and the ship's computer had obeyed voice commands. He felt a rush of relief, and keeping his voice down he spoke the necessary words: 'A-activate autopilot.'

'Access denied,' said the ship's computer.

'Please?' said Hal.

'Access denied.'

Hal frowned. The ship would only obey the pilot . . . or his voice, at any rate. There was no easy fix after all. Cautiously he scanned the instruments on the console, looking for one which said 'Autopilot'. Unfortunately they were all blank.

'What are we going to do?' hissed Stinky. 'Should we wake him up?'

Hal considered it, but he knew the punishment would be huge. Instead of camping, they'd probably spend the week in detention - or worse. If only he hadn't jogged the stupid controls! Then he got an idea. He'd touched the controls when he climbed down from the pilot's chair, so why not do the same thing again? If he got it exactly right, his fingers would brush the same controls, and the autopilot would come back on.

Hal climbed into the pilot's chair and put his hands on the console.

'You're not going to fly it?' muttered Stinky. 'Please, Hal. We're already –'

'Just watch,' said Hal. He swung the chair and put his hand firmly on the console, trying to duplicate his earlier movements. His fingers pressed on half a dozen buttons, and as he leapt down from the chair, the computer spoke:

'Airlocks sealed. Docking clamps activated. Landing lights on. Seatbelt warning signs on. Inflight movie terminated.'

'Oh no,' breathed Stinky. 'Hal, you've really done it now!'

— 7 —

Lessons

At that moment Hal noticed something missing. He turned this way and that, trying to work out what it was, and then it dawned on him. The pilot had stopped snoring!

'H-he's waking up,' muttered Stinky, who'd noticed the same thing.

The pilot started to roll over, and Hal eyed the door. Could they run out quickly before they were spotted?

No.

The pilot sat up, rubbing sleep from his eyes. He blinked once or twice, then frowned as he spotted Hal and Stinky. His gaze travelled from the boys, to the flight console, and back to the boys. The pilot had a mane of black hair and a neat goatee shot through with grey, and when he stood up he towered over the boys.

an explain,' said Hal.

ıııe pilot ignored him. 'Ann, set the autopilot.'

'Complying,' said the computer.

Hal glanced at the screen. The stars were now moving in the other direction, and the words 'Autopilot activated' were back. They weren't going to fly into a star, or return to the orbiter, which was good news. Unfortunately Hal and Stinky were in for a rough landing of their own. 'I'm sorry,' said Hal. 'We –'

'Don't worry about it,' said the pilot, with a casual wave of his hand. 'There's nothing to crash into out here.'

'But I –'

'You ever flown a ship before?'

'No.'

'Take a seat, both of you.'

Hal and Stinky exchanged a glance. They were expecting a huge telling off, but the pilot didn't seem to mind them being there. 'Are you sure? I mean, we should probably get back to the lounge.'

'Go on, hop up.' The pilot addressed the computer again. 'Ann, show 'em the one about the aliens and the teleporter network.'

'Complying.'

For a moment Hal thought they were going to

watch a movie, then realised 'them' meant the rest of the group in the passenger lounge.

'That'll keep them quiet for a bit,' said the pilot. 'Now, let's start your flying lesson. The first thing you have to remember is this: a spaceship is nothing like an aeroplane. When you point the nose of an aircraft, the rest of the plane tends to follow. So, if you pull back on the stick, the nose goes up and the plane climbs. However, no matter where you point a spaceship, it keeps hurtling along in the same direction. When you use the controls you're just spinning the ship around, and the only way to get it to move on the new heading is to fire the thrusters. Is that clear?'

Stinky nodded. Hal shook his head.

'Ann, show them the flight dynamics video.'

'Complying.'

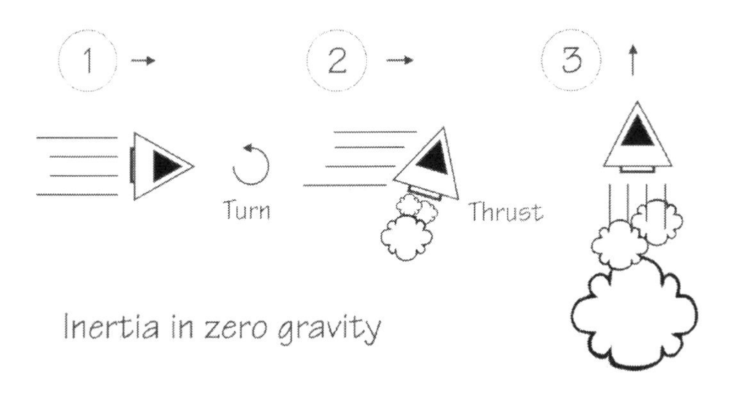

Hal watched the animation and understood

immediately. Why couldn't Teacher show them videos to explain math problems? That would make school work so much easier!

'Got it now?' asked the pilot.

Hal nodded.

'Okay. Ann, turn the autopilot off.'

'Autopilot deactivated.'

'Why is your computer called Ann?' asked Stinky.

'Tell him, Ann.'

'I'm a node in the Automated Nagivation Network, or ANN for short.'

'She's connected to the local navigational system,' said the pilot. 'She knows where we are at all times.'

'Can you . . . can you jump between stars?'

'Not this tub. It's strictly a local ferry. Of course, a few years back . . . ' The pilot's voice tailed off and he stared at the screen, lost in thought.

Hal finally remembered his manners. 'Um, what's your name?' he asked.

The pilot blinked, then stuck out his hand. 'Kent Spearman at your service.'

Hal and Stinky introduced themselves. 'How come you didn't tell us off?' asked Stinky. 'We could have flown your ship right into the sun!'

Spearman shrugged. 'Ann's controlling the ship. She'd stop any funny business like that.'

'But we're not supposed to be here.'

Hal wanted to clamp his hand over Stinky's mouth. Was his friend trying to get them punished?

However, Kent didn't seem to mind. 'If it was that important I'd have locked the door. Truth is, I often let passengers into the flight deck. Space can get pretty boring.'

'Have you flown a lot?' asked Hal.

'Absolutely. I used to run a passenger liner called the Luna Rose. Then there was a freighter called the Tiger.'

Hal started. 'But . . . I know that one! The Tiger was damaged, and we joined it to the space station.'

Spearman shook his head. 'It wouldn't be the same one. Tiger is a common name . . . I guess people like strong names for their ships. You don't get many Fluffies or Bunnies.'

Hal winced at the thought. Imagine a spaceship called the Fluffy Bunny! You'd be laughed at wherever you went.

'You can go too far the other way,' said Spearman.

‘I knew a guy once, he had a ship called the Volante. Talk about pretentious!’

‘What’s pretun . . . pretin . . . ’

‘Show off,’ said Stinky.

‘I am not!’ said Hal indignantly.

‘No, the word. Pretentious means show off.’

‘Correct.’ Spearman smiled. ‘He was called Hal too. It’s funny, but you even look a bit like him.’

Hal wasn’t interested in old pilots. He wanted to fly the ship! ‘So how do you loop the loop in this thing?’

‘Let’s try a few basic exercises first.’

Hal frowned. That was one of Teacher’s favourite phrases, and the exercises were never basic!

‘Stephen, you go first. Move the controls to port - that’s left - and keep an eye on the heading indicator. If you push too far the bubble will go into the red zone, and that puts a strain on the ship.’

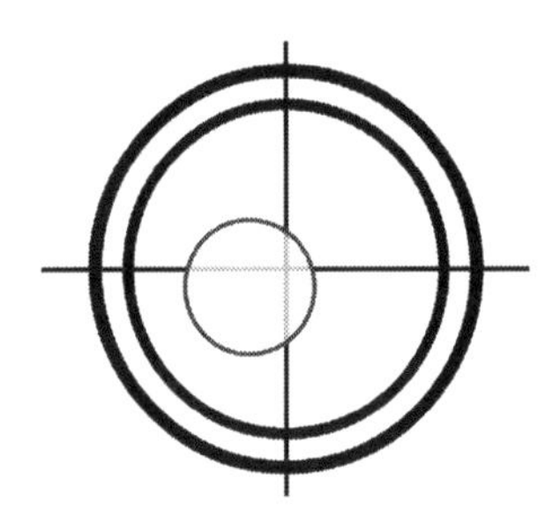

Stinky did as he was told, and the nose of the ship swung to the left.

'Good. Now your turn, Hal. Try moving the ship the other way.'

Hal took hold of the flight controls. The plastic was cool to the touch, and the grips were worn where pilots had spent countless hours flying the old ship. They were heavy, but they moved smoothly to the right. The stars on the main screen slowed down, stopped, then slid across the screen in the opposite direction. He was doing it! He was flying the ship!

'Good. Now let's try –'

'Status warning,' said Ann suddenly. 'Temperature spike in the starboard engine.'

Spearman reacted instantly, hauling Stinky out of the co-pilot's chair so he could take his place. His fingers flew over the controls and his eyes scanned the displays and status screens. Hal was impressed by his skill, although he was less certain about the worried look on the pilot's face. In fact, Spearman was frantically using the controls as though their lives depended on it.

'Sorry lads, lesson's over. You'll have to go back to the passenger lounge.'

'Is there a problem?'

'Nothing I can't handle. Now go!'

Hal slid out of the chair, and he and Stinky retreated to the back of the flight deck. From behind, Spearman looked like a hyperactive octopus playing three piano concertos at once - his arms flew over the console, and streams of text zoomed across the main screen. A lot of the writing was in red, and Hal couldn't help noticing words like 'Error' and 'Warning' and 'Danger'.

'I said go!' shouted Kent, when he realised they were still there.

Hal and Stinky fled, and the flight deck door thudded to behind them.

— 8 —

Lifeboats

Hal and Stinky went back to the lounge, where they sneaked back to their seats under cover of darkness. The movie looked pretty cool, with a fleet of huge alien ships chasing one little fighter in and out of an asteroid field. The fighter jinked left, and Hal gasped as a burst of gunfire shattered a rock, blowing fragments across the screen with a loud 'boom!'

There was a second explosion, and this time the whole floor shook. Hal grinned in delight as smoke drifted across the screen. Talk about realistic special effects! It even stank like a real fire!

At that moment the screen went dark. Dim red emergency lights came on, and several people cried out in alarm. Hal glanced at Stinky, who was flapping at the smoke with both hands. 'What do you think happened?'

'Some kind of power failure,' said Stinky. 'We should probably –'

Hal never found out what his friend was going to suggest, because at that moment Kent Spearman's voice crackled through the overhead speakers.

'This is your pilot speaking. Folks, we have a small problem in the engine bay. It's nothing to worry about, but I'd like you to make your way to the escape pods right now. And whatever you do, don't forget to –'

The speaker and the emergency lighting cut out at the exact same moment, leaving the passenger lounge in total darkness. 'Don't forget to what?' shouted a voice nearby.

Several people cried out in panic, and Hal decided to take charge. 'Listen up. Me and Stinky know where the escape pods are. Follow us, and we'll lead you right to them.'

There were lots of cries of 'how?' and 'no chance!', but Hal and Stinky managed to convince the doubters. They opened the double doors, and the corridor light outside flickered and flashed like a red strobe. For a moment Hal suspected the lift might be out of action, and he was relieved to see the control panel shining with a steady glow. Unfortunately, they would need three or four trips to get everyone down to the next deck. 'Stinky, you take the first lot,' said Hal importantly. 'Show them how the pods work and get them seated. And remember, don't put anyone in that broken pod.'

Stinky nodded, and between them they guided the first batch into the lift. The four parent volunteers hung back, trying to comfort some of the smaller children.

'Don't worry,' said Hal, as the lift doors closed. 'I've met the pilot. He knows exactly what to do.'

The lift came back empty, and Hal herded the next group of children in. Once the doors closed there were only six people left, including himself, Stinky and two of the adults.

'How do you know so much about the ship?' asked a short, balding man. He was comforting his daughter, a girl called Natalie who often gave Hal grief in class.

'I . . . studied the plans.' Hal glanced towards the flight deck doors.

'Like *you* ever studied anything,' said Natalie.

Her dad shushed her. 'This young man is helping.'

'Like *he* ever helped anyone,' muttered Natalie, quieter this time.

Hal made a face at her, and then the lift came back and he waved everyone on board. 'Stinky, show them to the escape pods.'

'What about you?'

'I have to do something.'

Natalie's dad frowned. 'We're not leaving you behind. Get in.'

Hal didn't have time to argue. He stepped into the lift, pressed the middle button, and stepped out again just before the doors snapped together. Then, as the lift carried others away, he hurried to the flight deck. Inside, Kent Spearman was still working the controls. The main screen was almost entirely covered in red, and alarms whined and buzzed and clattered from the console.

'What are you doing here?' demanded the pilot. 'I told you to clear out!'

'I came to help.'

'What can you do?' Spearman gestured at the screen. 'This thing is toast!'

'Is the ship going to crash?'

'No, there's nothing to hit out here.'

'Why the panic then?'

'One of the engines blew up, and the other one's on fire. The extinguishers failed, and ten minutes from now this entire ship will be a smoking ruin.'

Hal gulped.

'I'm about to launch the escape pods,' said Kent. 'You need to be on one.'

'What about you?'

'My job is to fight the fire. There's still a tiny chance, but if that fails I'll be taking the last pod.'

There was a terrific explosion, and Hal was knocked off his feet. A siren wailed, and as he got up again he saw 'Abandon Ship!' plastered across the main screen in blood-red letters.

'You should have left earlier,' muttered Spearman. 'Ann, launch the pods.'

'Complying.'

There was a moment of silence and then . . . *whoosh - whoosh - whoosh!* The ship rocked as the lifepods were ejected, and Hal caught a glimpse of the gleaming white cylinders hurtling away from the ship on the main screen.

'Time to go,' said Spearman.

'Please . . . take care of yourself, captain.'

'It's not goodbye, Ann.' Spearman patted his pocket. 'I have your backup right here.'

Hal followed him out of the flight deck. The smoke was thicker now, and he coughed several times while they were waiting for the lift. 'I thought you weren't supposed to use lifts when there was a fire?' he asked.

Spearman nodded. 'Normally that's right, but this is a special lift. It has its own power supply, and it's driven by anti-gravity. Do you know what that is?'

Hal knew all right. It wasn't that long ago he'd used an anti-gravity cannon to shoot down an enemy ship*.

The lift arrived and Spearman bustled him inside.

'What if they took all the pods?' asked Hal.

'There's one left.' Spearman reached into his flightsuit and took out a rag. He tore it in two and gave Hal half. 'Stick that over your mouth, and try not to breathe too deeply.'

The doors opened on an empty corridor. The smoke was even thicker here, and even with the rag over his face Hal found it really hard to breathe. There was a glow at the far end of the corridor, and he realised the floor was giving off waves of heat. Somewhere below a fire was raging, and they didn't have much time left.

Spearman stopped at the doors to the pod bays. Both were wide open, and Hal could see all the pod launchers from the corridor. The left hand

---

* *Hal Junior: The Secret Signal*

ones were empty, and the displays showed 'Pod Launched' in flashing orange letters. He glanced to the right and saw the same. Then he looked closer and realised the display on the far left wasn't orange . . . it was red. Instead of 'Pod Launched' it was showing 'Pod Fault'. 'Er, Mr Spearman?'

'Yes Hal?'

'Do you have any other escape pods?'

— 9 —

Left behind

Kent Spearman frowned at the display. 'That was working last week. What happened to it?'

'It wasn't me,' said Hal quickly. He was used to getting the blame but this time - for once - it wasn't his fault.

Spearman hurried from one pod launcher to the next, double-checking the displays. 'Not good,' he said at last.

Smoke swirled around, and Hal could feel the heat of the fire through his shoes. 'A-are we stranded?'

'No, not at all.' Spearman thumped his fist on the 'Pod Faulty' display. There was a spit and a crackle, and the red text disappeared. At first Hal thought the pilot had fixed it, but then he saw Spearman's worried expression. Obviously things weren't going to plan.

Spearman took out a pocket knife and levered the

control panel off the wall, exposing a tangle of wires. He poked around, then jumped and swore as one of them gave him a shock.

'It's a shame Stinky isn't here,' said Hal. 'He's really good with electronics.'

'Lucky for him he isn't,' muttered Spearman, shaking his fingers. Then he glanced at Hal. 'Do you really think he could help?'

'Stinky knows everything,' said Hal simply.

'We'd better speak to him.' Spearman crossed to the opposite wall, where there was a computer terminal. He touched his finger to the security pad, then leant close to the speaker. 'Ann, can you tell me which pod Stinky is in?'

'Negative,' said the ship's computer. 'Stinky unknown. Name is not on the passenger list.'

'Stephen,' said Hal. 'Stephen Binn.'

Spearman repeated this, and the screen zoomed in on a white cylinder. It was tumbling away from the passenger ship, and it looked tiny against the star-filled sky. Within seconds Spearman had set up communications, and Stinky's owlish face looked out of the screen. He was a nasty shade of green, and he seemed to be swallowing a lot.

'Are you all right?' asked Hal.

'Y-yeah. Just a bit dizzy.' Stinky started to float away, and Hal laughed as his friend flapped his arms wildly.

'Stephen, this is Kent Spearman. Can you hear me?'

'Yes Mr Spearman.'

'Hal says you're a whizz with electronics.'

Stinky swam back into view. 'It's one of my favourite subjects.'

Hal snorted. Every subject was one of Stinky's favourites!

'Do you know how to override a keypad?' asked Spearman.

'Which model?'

Spearman glanced at Hal. 'Can you check?'

'It'll be on the bottom of the cover,' called Stinky.

Hal hurried across the pod bay, bursting with importance. He was helping to save everyone! Well, save the pilot and himself, anyway. He found the cover on the floor and picked it up. 'KL-91,' he called out.

Stinky closed his eyes, and Hal could almost hear the whirr of his incredible brain. Any second now his friend would have the answer. Any second now.

Instead, Stinky shook his head. 'I'm sorry, I don't know that model. Do you think it's similar to the KL-90?'

'How should I know?' snapped Hal.

'Let's assume they are,' continued Stinky, still

thinking hard. He started to drift away again, but before he was out of sight his eyes snapped open. 'Cut the orange wire, and twist the green and purple ones together.'

'Cut orange, twist purple and green,' muttered Spearman. 'Thanks!'

'B-before you go . . . ' began Stinky.

'Yes?'

'Is there any way to stop the pod spinning so much?'

'Just wait until the boosters kick in.' Spearman cut the connection and hurried over to the control panel. He pulled at the wires until the orange, green and purple ones were all sticking out. Unfortunately there were two purple ones. 'Well that's just great,' muttered Spearman.

'What happens if you join the wrong ones? Will it blow up?'

'No, but it might seal the door for good.' Spearman hesitated, then followed Stinky's instructions, snipping the orange wire before stripping and twisting the rest together. In the end, he joined both the purple ones to the green one. There was a brief hesitation and then . . . success! The door started to open.

Boom!

Something exploded below decks, and the force

threw Hal to the floor. He wasn't down long . . . as soon as he felt the searing heat on his hands he bounced right up again. Then he realised the smoke had vanished, and there was a distant whistling sound.

'Are you all right?' shouted Spearman.

Hal could hardly breathe and he certainly couldn't speak. Instead, he nodded.

'Hull breach,' yelled Spearman. 'Air's going. Have to get . . . in.'

Unfortunately the door to the escape pod had only opened five or six centimetres, and then jammed. Hal could see into the pod through the gap, and it looked cosy and welcoming.

Spearman put both hands on the edge of the door and braced his feet on the wall. He heaved with all his might but the door didn't budge. 'Help . . . me . . . open!' shouted Spearman, his voice thin and his face red with the strain.

Hal put his shoulder to the door and jammed one foot against the wall. There was an exercise in the Space Station gym where they had to lean into a padded wall and push it clear across the room. Hal always finished first, even after Stinky sat on the opposite side of the wall with two friends. Unfortunately, the pod door wasn't padded, and it was harder to budge than a wall with the entire class perched on top.

Hal put all his strength into a huge push, and the door gave. There was a moment of weightlessness, and then he and Spearman tumbled into the escape pod. The inner door closed smartly, and Spearman was at the controls before Hal could reach for the safety belt.

Whoooooosh!

Hal was pressed down into his seat as the pod shot away from the damaged passenger ship. It was an effort just to raise his arms, but he managed to buckle in. The crushing weight eased, and before long it was gone. Now they were weightless, and Hal's stomach began to turn somersaults. No wonder Stinky had looked as green as a head of broccoli!

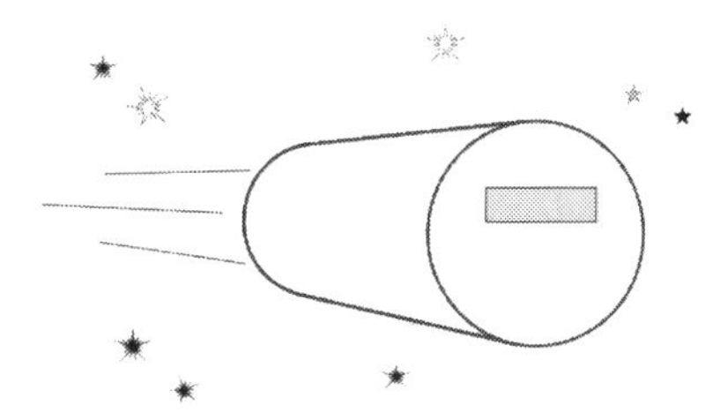

— 10 —

In flight

Kent Spearman loosened his straps so he could reach the central control panel. He changed a few settings, steadying the capsule, and then he fired the boosters. The thrust from the engines pressed Hal into his seat, and he breathed a sigh of relief as gravity returned. It was only weak, but it was enough to orient himself.

Spearman glanced at him. 'I wouldn't celebrate yet,' he said, his voice grave. 'We're not out of the woods.'

Hal was mystified. How could they be in the woods when there weren't any trees?

Kent saw his puzzled expression. 'We've escaped one danger, but there are plenty more. For example, if the ship explodes it might take this pod with it. On the other hand, I could burn all our fuel getting the pod to a safe distance, and then we'd have none left for landing.'

Hal remembered his friends. 'What about the others? Will they know what to do?'

'They got clear sooner than we did, so they're further away.' Spearman tapped a small display, and Hal saw the other pods strung out like pearls on a necklace. There was a pulsing red dot in the middle of the screen, with a much larger circle drawn around it. Just inside the big circle was a lonely white dot. 'That's us,' said Spearman, pointing to the white dot.

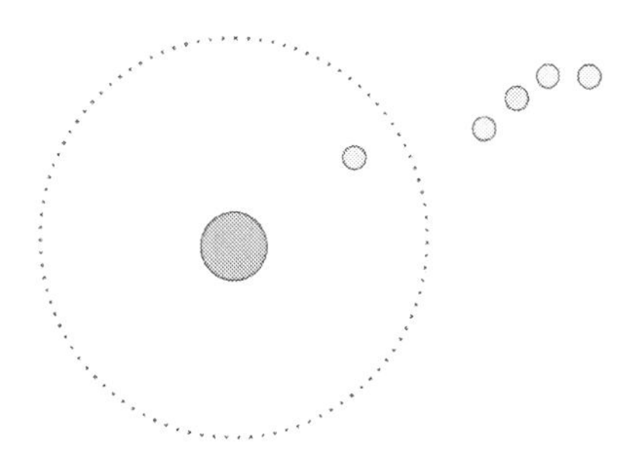

'What's that dotted circle?'

'The blast radius. When the ship explodes, everything inside that circle will be destroyed.'

'But . . . we're inside the circle!'

'Correct, which is why our thruster is going full throttle. I'm trying to get as far away from the wreck as possible, before it blows up.'

Hal watched the screen, his eyes wide. The little white dot was crawling towards the edge of the circle, while the red dot in the middle pulsed faster and faster. 'Will it blow us up?'

'Of course not!'

Hal remembered a visit to the sickbay once, after he'd cut his knee on a metal staircase. He'd asked the medic whether the treatment was going to hurt, and she'd said 'of course not!' in exactly the same tone of voice. The treatment did hurt - a lot - and the experience taught him that adults often said the opposite of what they meant. Instead of listening to their words you had to study their faces, and Kent Spearman's was tense and worried.

'Bang!' shouted Hal, and Spearman almost fell off his chair.

'Little horror,' muttered the pilot, as he recovered. Then he shot Hal a quick grin. 'All right, I won't lie to you. We're in for a rough ride, but I'm pretty sure we'll make it. These capsules can take a lot of punishment.'

'Have you escaped a wreck before?'

'Oh, yes. Several.' Spearman laughed at Hal's expression. 'It's not like I crash them on purpose. Things just . . . happen.'

'Will you tell me about one?'

'Sure. I had a close call once on planet Forzen, where they filled my ship with contaminated fuel. The engines barely had enough thrust to get me off the ground, and they kept cutting out. It was touch and go, I can tell you, but I made it.'

'And what about the crashes?'

'Maybe later, eh?' Spearman studied the display, where the white dot was almost clear of the circle. 'Looks like we –'

CLANG!

Something smashed into the capsule, sending it tumbling through space. More impacts followed, and Hal clung to the safety belt for dear life, squeezing his eyes shut. The capsule bounced and shook until Hal didn't know which way was up. It was like sitting inside a tin can getting tumbled around in a giant concrete mixer full of rocks.

The crashes and bangs tailed off at last, and Hal opened one eye. They were okay! They'd made it!

Spearman smiled at him and patted the wall. 'I told you these things were strong.'

'Why didn't we hear the explosion?' demanded Hal.

'There's no sound in space, Hal. The only reason you heard those bits and pieces hitting the pod is because it's full of air.' Spearman held a hand out, his fingers clenched in a fist. 'When the ship went off it sent pieces flying every which way.' He opened his hand, splaying his fingers. 'Some of them hit us, but they didn't do any damage.'

'You mean we're okay?'

'Sure.'

'And the others?'

Spearman inspected the display. 'All present and correct.' Then he looked closer. 'Oh dear.'

'What's the matter?'

'Your friend Stinky . . . his capsule has five people in it.'

'Is that bad?'

Kent nodded. 'The pods are only rated for four.'

'Stinky's not very big,' said Hal. 'He should be all right.'

'It's not that. There are only four sets of belts.' Kent used the central console and Hal felt the engines firing again.

'What are you doing?'

'We'll have to link up in space and transfer one of them across. It's risky, but there's no choice. I've told their capsule to slow down so we can dock with it.'

Hal watched the screen, and he saw two white dots getting closer and closer. They joined as one, and the capsule shook with a thud. Kent got up and opened the airlock and Hal saw right into the second capsule, with five worried faces looking back at him. Kent had already sent them a message, telling them the plan, and Stinky was through the airlock before any of the others could move.

'Best of luck,' called Kent, and he sealed the door again. There was a grating sound as the pods separated, and then the second pod fired its thrusters, moving to a safe distance.

'We don't want to land on top of them,' explained Kent. 'They have more fuel than us, so they can make the course change.'

Meanwhile, Hal helped Stinky with the belts, strapping him in tight before Kent could do it for him. When the pilot checked Stinky's belts, he nodded his approval. 'Nicely done, Hal.'

Hal beamed to himself.

'Okay boys,' said Kent Spearman. 'Here's the sitrep.'

'That's situation report,' murmured Stinky.

'I know!' protested Hal, even though he didn't.

Kent ignored the interruptions. 'We have plenty of fuel left for landing, and we should set down in about eight hours.'

Eight hours! Hal cleared his throat. 'Er, Mr Spearman?'

'Yes?'

'Where's the bathroom?'

— 11 —

Are we there yet?

To Hal, eight hours cooped up in the capsule felt more like eight weeks. He soon tired of using the emergency toilet, and Spearman wouldn't let him touch the food supplies in case they needed them to survive. Stinky curled up and went to sleep, although Hal suspected he was just pretending so he didn't have to listen to his complaints. Hal woke him up several times to check, until Kent told him to stop.

Hal assumed the pods would be collected by a rescue ship, scooping them up in space like a fishing boat filling its nets. However, Spearman explained that planet Gyris only had one emergency vessel . . . and it was being repaired. That meant the pods would have to land on the planet by themselves. Worse, landing was automatic, and there was no way to choose your destination. They might land in the middle of a desert, or on top of a mountain, or splash down in the sea. According to Kent, if that happened you just bobbed around on the ocean, getting very seasick while rescue ships looked for you.

With six pods scattered all over the planet, it would take the authorities some time to reach them all. Hal suddenly realised they might spend the entire camping trip living out of the escape pod, drinking canned water and eating stale ration bars. It was so unfair. They might as well have stayed aboard the Space Station!

Hal glanced up. He'd just noticed a thin whistling noise, which sounded exactly like an air leak.

'Don't worry,' said Spearman. 'We're entering the planet's atmosphere. You'd better tighten your belts, though.'

Hal woke Stinky, again, and they did as they were told. The whistling got louder, and the tiny capsule began to shake. There were bumps too, as though they were hitting something. 'Are those clouds?'

'No, we're too high up for those. It's just variations in atmospheric density.'

'Uh-huh?'

'Sorry. Pockets of air at different temperatures. It's like flying through soup and hitting a piece of carrot or potato.'

Hal imagined a giant bowl of stew with a spaceship splatting through the ingredients. His stomach growled, and he remembered he hadn't eaten for hours.

The whistling became a steady roar, and the air in the capsule began to heat up. It was just starting to get uncomfortably warm when there was a loud Fsssh! right under their feet, making Hal jump. 'What was that?'

'Re-entry shield,' said Spearman calmly. 'Without it, we'd burn up like a pan full of bacon.'

Hal was beginning to wish Kent would pick different examples. Something which didn't involve food would be good. He also wished the pilot would explain things before they happened, not afterwards. 'What next?'

'We'll fall for a while, and then the thrusters will slow us down for landing. When that happens your head will feel like it's three or four times heavier than usual. It's like taking a slice of cake and –'

'I get the idea,' said Hal quickly. It was hot in the capsule, and burning air was still roaring by outside. Hal imagined the pod dropping through the atmosphere like a meteor, trailing a long, fiery streamer. What would it look like to the people on the ground? Would they think they were under attack? Were they getting ready to shoot the capsule out of the sky?

He was still dreaming up exciting disasters when the thrusters fired, adding their deep rumble to all the other noises. It was like someone standing on the brakes, and Hal gasped at the crushing weight. It was an effort to keep his head up, and he wished he could lie down and rest. Unfortunately, the seat belts held him to the chair, keeping him upright.

'Not . . . long . . . now.' Spearman spoke with effort, the muscles in his neck standing out.

A few minutes later, the roaring air tailed off, but the thrusters kept up their rumble. Spearman reached for the console, and the screen displayed a bird's-eye view of the ground. Hal could see green from one side of the display to the other, and as they dropped further he realised they were all trees. There were several hills, which made the ground look like a lumpy green carpet, and in the distance he could see a big mountain range. There was a river, too, winding between the trees like a gleaming silver ribbon.

A cursor darted around the screen, pausing on shadows before moving on. 'What's it doing?' asked Hal.

'The pod's trying to find a landing spot.'

Hal realised they were talking normally. The thrusters were quieter now, and his head was back to its normal weight again. 'What if it can't find one?'

'We'll have to take our chances between the trees,' said Spearman.

Hal scanned the small screen. There was no sign of the other capsules, but they might have landed in the trees too. If so, they'd be under the canopy and invisible from the air. 'How will the rescue teams find us?'

'Every pod has a beacon. It started transmitting the second we left the passenger ship. All they have to do is track it.'

'Will it take long?'

Spearman shook his head.

‘What’s going to happen to you? I mean, you lost your ship.’

‘Don’t worry, it was insured.’

‘But what about your job?’

‘Pilots are always in demand.’

‘I’m going to be a pilot one day,’ said Hal.

Spearman ruffled his hair. ‘And I bet you’ll be a good one, too.’

Roar!

The thrusters fired one last time, slowing them for the landing. Hal saw the trees coming up to meet them, and then he heard branches grinding on the hull. The pod tilted sideways, and there was a moment of weightlessness before . . . oof!

They landed with a thud, right on their side, and Hal saw stars as his head whacked the padded chair. The lights went out, leaving them in darkness, but before he could panic the door slid open. Hal’s first view of planet Gyris was a big tree towering over the pod, with sunlight filtering through the leaves. There was noise too . . . chirps and tweets by the thousand, wind rustling in the trees, and the click-click-click of the cooling jets.

Then there were the smells! Freshly disturbed earth, sap from the broken branches, and a vast background smell of . . . planet. Hal took a deep breath and closed his eyes, savouring the variety.

As Kent Spearman would say, it was like eating dry bread your whole life, and then discovering chocolate cake.

— 12 —

Roll, roll, roll the lifeboat

Kent rubbed his head and sat up. 'Well, we made it.'

'Where are we?' asked Hal.

'About a thousand kilometres from the nearest settlement. They're on the coast, and we're inland.'

'Are there any wild animals?'

'Only if we landed on them.' Spearman laughed at Hal's expression. 'No, nothing bigger than a rabbit.'

'Do they have those here?'

'They have rabbits everywhere,' said Kent.

Hal glanced up at the doorway, which was like a skylight in the roof. It was a long way up, and he realised they couldn't actually reach it. 'How are we going to get out?'

'Not sure yet.' Spearman frowned. 'We'll need to rig a cover for that in case it rains.'

Hal remembered rain from a documentary. 'Is that when water falls from the sky?'

'Correct.' Spearman rapped on the wall. 'A good downpour could fill this up, and we'll be swimming around like goldfish in a bowl.'

'Why don't we close the door?'

'We can pull it to, but we can't seal it. We need fresh air.'

'Can't we roll the pod over?' asked Stinky.

'Not without a crane.'

'What about using the thrusters?'

Spearman hesitated, rubbing his chin. 'It could be dangerous. They're very powerful, and the jets could start a fire.'

'But it might work?'

'We'll see. First we need to look around outside. For all we know there might be a building out there, or other people.'

Hal thought this extremely unlikely, but he knew Spearman was right. If they fired the engines the heat would burn anything around the ship. However, they still had another problem to deal with: getting out of the pod. 'Is there a ladder?'

'No, I'll boost you up. Come on, on your feet.'

A few moments later they were ready. Hal stood on the console, then stepped onto Spearman's shoulders. He could just reach the door frame, and he hauled himself up, getting his elbows over the edge before tipping sideways to raise his knee.

'Be careful,' called Spearman, from the darkness below. 'Don't roll off.'

Hal got his knee on the edge of the frame and shifted sideways onto the hull. Now he was lying face-down on the pod, with the trees above him and the ground down below. He could see a thick carpet of brown leaves, with fresh green ones and broken branches scattered on top. Hal looked up and saw a ragged hole in the canopy where the pod had torn its way through.

Stinky joined him on top of the pod, and the boys exchanged a worried look.

'What can you see?' called Spearman.

'Trees,' shouted Hal. 'Lots and lots of them.'

'Can you get down to the ground?'

Hal peered over the edge, and discovered the capsule had come down on the side of a hill. The ground sloped away below him, the thick trees and undergrowth hiding the depths of the valley. He looked over his shoulder towards the top of the hill, but could only see a short distance through the dense woods.

Then he looked along the capsule, and he saw a tree bent sideways under the weight of the hull. If he could grab hold of that, he could swing on it and reach the ground that way. 'I think I see a way down.'

'Just make sure you can get up again.'

Hal eyed the tree, studying the distance to the ground. It was bent over a long way, and it shouldn't be too hard to climb back up. 'I'll be right back,' he called. 'Wait there.'

Spearman muttered something, but Hal didn't catch the words.

◆

Hal shimmied across the hull to the tree, then took hold of the trunk with both hands. He was surprised to find it was smooth and cold to the touch, because he'd always thought living things were warm. Something else Teacher never told them!

It only took a moment to reach the ground, where his shoes sank into the spongy earth. It was like the mats in the gym, except his shoes left muddy footprints. 'Come on, Stinky. It's easy.'

His friend peered over the edge, then came down nervously, as though he'd never climbed a tree in his life. Then Hal realised . . . neither of them had!

'That wasn't too hard,' he said, brushing his hands on his clothes.

'Just wait until we have to climb up again,' muttered Stinky.

The boys looked around, peering through the trees. The ground sloped away, and thick bushes made it hard to see very far. Hal couldn't see any of the other capsules, and he certainly couldn't hear anyone over the bird and insect noises. Somewhere in the distance there was a crack and a thud as a branch fell off a tree, and Hal glanced up fearfully. How often did trees drop bits on you, and was there any warning? When they finally started camping, he decided his tent was going to be right out in the open.

But never mind camping - they'd left Kent Spearman inside the capsule. How were they going to get him out? Obviously there wasn't any rope around, nor any ladders. Old jungle movies always had swinging creepers hanging from every tree, but there were none to be seen here.

Hal looked back at the capsule, and his eyes narrowed. The pod had knocked several branches off when it came down, and a few were trapped underneath. What if he pushed a branch down inside the capsule - could Mr Spearman climb out?

He ducked under the capsule and tugged at one of the branches. Unfortunately the entire weight of the capsule was resting on it, and it wouldn't budge. He was on the lower side of the slope too, below the capsule, which made it even harder to pull a branch out.

'Hal!' whispered Stinky. 'I can hear . . . water.'

'Water?'

The boys noticed a gap between the bushes, and further down the slope they saw a natural rock wall with real water splashing from an underground stream. They hurried to look, Kent Spearman completely forgotten.

Water - real water! - was trickling between two large rocks and running down the rock wall. Water was scarce aboard the Space Station, where they were only allowed to use it for drinking. They didn't have showers or baths . . . they had to use a special force field which removed dirt from anything it touched. Unfortunately, it felt like sandpaper, and it left your skin red and tingly.

Hal crouched and put his hand into the stream, and he couldn't help grinning as the icy cold liquid ran over his fingers. He stared at it, amazed that so much water could just bubble up from the ground and go to waste.

The wall was about a metre and a half high, and Hal's eyes narrowed as he saw the shallow pool at the foot. 'We should build that up a bit. Make a dam.'

Stinky nodded, his eyes shining.

They clambered down the wall, and Hal took a big scoop of dirt and heaped it across the stream. The water ran either side, making new streams, and Stinky added another couple of handfuls. Before long there was a deeper pool of water, and the boys were just planning an even bigger dam when Hal remembered the pod . . . and Mr Spearman. 'Stinky, we'd better go.'

Guiltily, they both stood up, and then they realised their hands were covered in mud. Hal looked at the sticky mess, wondering how to clean it off, and then he laughed as he spotted the pool. He crouched alongside it and did something he hadn't been able to do since he'd moved to the Space Station as a four-year-old: he washed his hands in water. Then, daringly, he splashed some in his face, and he grinned at the refreshing, cold feel.

'Hal, why don't you help Mr Spearman while I build the dam? We don't know how long we're going to be trapped here, and we'll need somewhere to wash.'

Hal frowned. *He* wanted to build the dam too, but rescuing the pilot was an important job. 'Okay, it's a deal. But make sure you do it right!'

Hal made his way up the slope to the pod, ducking his head as he rounded the nose to get to the upper part of the slope. He spotted several large branches straight way, and while most were trapped under the pod, one moved when he put his weight on it. The wood creaked and groaned but it wouldn't come free. Then Hal tried lifting it, and he felt the wood shifting. Excellent! He bent his knees, straightened his back and imagined he was in the finals of the Intergalactic Weight Lifting competition.

The crowd held its breath as Hal Junior, youngest competitor in the history of the sport, took to the stage. He bowed to the Emperor and all the princes and princesses, basking in the royal applause. He spat on his hands and rubbed them together, then approached the weights and took a firm grip on the wooden barbell. A moment passed while he summoned all his energy, and then . . . three . . . two . . . one! He straightened his legs with an almighty heave.

The weight was immense! At first the barbell wouldn't budge, but Hal wasn't giving up. He took a deep breath and tried again, hauling on the wooden beam until it felt like his arms would come out of their sockets. Then, with a rush, he managed it.

Applause! Wild cheering! Whistles! The crowd went wild as Hal Junior lifted the huge weight! He'd done it!

The scene faded, and Hal discovered he was facing the pod with the branch in both hands. He felt pleased with himself, and he was about to take his prize back to Kent Spearman when he noticed something. Slowly, ever so slowly, the big tree holding the pod up was falling over. And slowly, ever so slowly, the huge escape pod was starting to roll away from him.

— 13 —

Shelter

Hal realised what had happened: the branch had been trapped under the pod, and had acted like a lever when he lifted it. The pod was resting on the side of a hill, and gravity was about to do its thing.

Then he realised the danger: Stinky was below the pod, working on the dam! If the pod rolled over him, he'd be squashed flat. Desperately he dropped the branch and put his hands on the side of the pod, but there was nothing to hold on to. Hal cupped his hands to his mouth and shouted as loudly as he could. 'Stinky!' he yelled, at the top of his voice. 'Lie down! NOW!' He took a deep breath and shouted again. 'Mr Spearman, HANG ON!'

The pod tipped further, and then it started to roll. Fallen branches cracked and splintered as the pod rolled over them, and the big tree went with a loud CRACK! Then . . . roll, roll, *roll* went the pod, crack

crack *crack!* went the trees, and oh-no-*no!* went Hal. The pod gathered speed, cutting a swathe through the forest as it bounded down the slope. Now and then it flew into the air, chopping trees off halfway up the trunks, and startled birds fled in every direction.

The pod finally came to a halt three or four hundred metres down the slope, resting against a stand of older trees. Hal ran to the waterfall, where he saw Stinky getting up from the pond, a stunned look on his face, water streaming from his clothes. Hal checked his friend was all right, then charged after the pod, clambering over fallen branches and struggling through flattened bushes. When he reached the pod, he could just see the top of the doorway, which was now face down and buried in the dirt. He got onto his hands and knees and started digging. 'Mr Spearman? Mr Spearman, are you okay?'

◆

Hal dug at the earth, making the hole bigger and bigger. He expected to meet the pilot digging from the other side, but he got all the way through on his own. When there was enough room he stuck his head through. 'Hello? Mr Spearman?'

'Hang . . . on.'

Hal's eyes adjusted to the darkness, and he looked around for the pilot. He couldn't see him at first, but then he looked up and saw him halfway up the wall, tangled in the seatbelts. 'Are you okay?'

'Of course I'm not okay! One minute I was sitting here using the computer, and the next someone turned the pod into a spin dryer.'

'It rolled down the hill.' Hal decided to skip his starring role. 'It was resting on some branches and one of them moved.'

'Well, look on the bright side. Now we won't have to build a cover for the door.'

Unless it starts rolling down the hill again, Hal thought to himself.

Stinky arrived, sopping wet and breathing hard. 'What happened?' he demanded.

'The tree fell over,' said Hal, leaving out all mention of weightlifting and levers.

Spearman got himself free and slid down the wall. He landed with a thump, and winced. 'That's not good.'

'Are you okay?' Hal asked him.

'No, I've twisted my ankle.'

Hal realised what that meant: They wouldn't be

able to walk out of there. 'Do you think the rescue teams will find us?'

'That was the plan, yes.' Spearman sat back against the wall, his face drawn. 'Hal, we're in a spot of trouble. I was just checking the computer over, and I found out the emergency beacon hasn't been transmitting. That means nobody knows where we are.'

'Can you switch it on?'

'No, it's burnt out.'

Hal thought for a moment. 'We could light a fire. People might see the smoke.'

'Yes, we'll need a fire all right. The other problem is food and water. We're short of both.'

'I found a stream,' said Hal. 'It's just up the hill.'

Spearman brightened. 'Good lads!'

Hal felt the warmth of a deed well done. 'We could dig the stream out a bit, and make it flow past the pod. That way you could get a drink without having to walk.'

'Thanks. That would be great.'

Hal felt a little less guilty about rolling the pod down the hill. It was his fault Mr Spearman was injured, and he was determined to make up for it.

'Okay, first things first,' said Kent. 'Let's make this doorway a little bigger, and then we'll check the computer for native plants and insects. There might be something growing around here we can survive on.' Spearman hesitated. 'Whatever you do, don't taste anything until you clear it with me. Understood?'

Hal nodded. Teacher had already warned the class several times, and his parents had reminded him too.

'Some plants are deadly poison, even if the leaves and berries look shiny and sweet. At best you could end up very ill. At worst . . . well, just be sure to clear them with me first.'

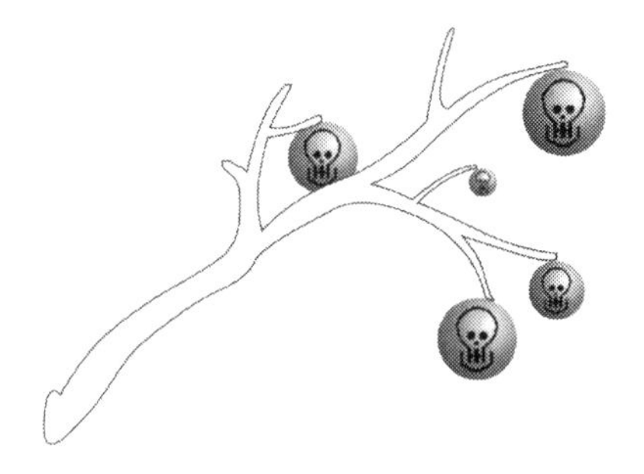

Spearman glanced at Stinky, who was wet and shivering. 'You're going to freeze. Let's see if we can find some dry clothes.'

Kent got Stinky to change into a pair of overalls from the escape pod. They were much too big for him, and with the arms and legs rolled up he looked like a circus clown. Then they all worked together on the doorway, clearing away the dirt until there was a decent tunnel. Water seeped into the bottom of the hole, and they would get very muddy clambering in and out. Spearman removed several of the padded seat cushions, laying them along the bottom of the tunnel. 'That'll keep the worst off.'

'Can we light a fire now?' asked Hal.

'See if you can find some wood. Look for dry leaves, twigs and branches. The green ones won't be any good.'

Hal and Stinky clambered through the tunnel to the outside. It seemed darker than before, and it was colder too. Hal realised night was falling, and unlike the Space Station, where they just dimmed the lights, here that meant total darkness. He suddenly felt very small amongst the trees.

He shook off the feeling and set off to find some wood. The pod had crashed through several trees on its way down the slope, but those were all green and growing, and Kent had explaincd that fresh wood wouldn't burn. Fortunately, one or two of the shattered trees had been dead, and those had littered the ground with brittle branches. It only took a few minutes to gather an armful, and then they staggered back to the pod.

Kent Spearman was sitting on a tree trunk, and Hal saw him wet his finger and hold it up in the air.

'What are you doing?'

'Checking the wind direction. If we build the fire in the wrong place, the smoke will blow straight into the capsule.'

Hal was impressed. He'd have built the fire right in front of the door, and he'd never given any thought to the smoke. He realised he had a lot to learn, and he was grateful Mr Spearman was there. Imagine if he'd come down in the woods on his own, or just him and Stinky! Then he remembered the others. Would they be eating poisoned berries and trying to light fires with green wood? 'Do you think everyone else will be okay?'

Spearman was busy snapping wood into smaller pieces, building them into a pile with the smallest bits on the bottom. 'Their beacons were fine,' he said at last. 'I bet they're tucked up in a nice hotel by now.'

Stinky looked worried. 'They will look for us, won't they? The rescue people, I mean?'

'Of course!' Spearman took out a firestarter and held the steady flame to the pile of wood. Nothing happened for a moment or two, and then the smaller twigs caught and flames spread through the pile. 'That reminds me . . . you should gather a pile of green leaves. If you hear a jet or a rescue copter, throw them on the fire.'

'Won't that put it out?'

'No, it'll make a huge amount of white smoke. They'll spot it right away.'

'Unless it's night time.'

'Correct. If it's dark, throw dry branches on to make the flames bigger. Something with lots of old leaves on.'

'Green leaves in the daytime, dry leaves at night.'

'You've got it.' Spearman glanced at the sky. 'Can you fetch some more wood? I don't know how cold it's going to be overnight, so we'd better lay in a good supply.'

Cold! Hal hadn't thought of that. Aboard the Space Station you just turned a dial and the climate control did the rest. He knew about snow and ice, of course, but he hadn't actually thought about sleeping outdoors, in real weather.

'Don't look so worried,' said Spearman. 'We have food, water and warmth. By tomorrow those rescue teams will be combing the forest, and we'll be back to civilisation in no time.'

Hal nodded.

'Listen, I saw a roll of fishing line in the emergency kit. Once you've got the wood I'll show you how to make a bow and arrows. How about that?'

'Really?' Hal's eyes widened. 'Can I go hunting?'

'Maybe just the trees, for now.' Spearman looked into the flames, and Hal could almost read his thoughts. If they weren't rescued soon, hunting and fishing might be the only way to survive!

— 14 —

Bow done

Hal and Stinky traipsed up and down the hill, fetching armfuls of wood, and by the time it got dark their legs were aching like crazy. Hal dumped the final load of branches onto the pile and sat down on a log. Mr Spearman had built the fire to a roaring blaze, and the warmth soon dealt with Hal's frozen nose and ears.

Spearman passed them a ration bar each, and Hal chomped his down in seconds. It hardly made a dent in his hunger, but a big drink of water helped. Then he noticed Spearman sorting through the pile of firewood. The pilot selected several straight branches, bending each one before setting them aside. When he had half a dozen he limped back to the log and sat down.

'How's your ankle?' asked Hal.

'Not too bad, thanks.' Spearman pulled up the leg

of his flightsuit, revealing a neat bandage. 'I can move around a bit, but I wouldn't want to walk far on it.'

'Are you making a bow?'

'Yes, I'll make a couple of them. Hopefully one of them will work.' Spearman took out a large pocket knife and cut notches at each end of the poles. Then he unwound several metres of fishing line. 'Do you know how to plait?'

Hal shook his head. As far as he knew, it was something you did with hair.

'This stuff isn't strong enough for a bowstring, but it'll be okay if we plait it.' Spearman measured off two metres of fishing line, then cut another dozen lengths the same. 'We'll double-plait it, six strands to a string. Here, take these.'

Hal was given six lengths of fishing line. They kept curling up, and before he knew it there was a big tangle in his lap.

'Tie the end off like this.' Spearman demonstrated, and Hal copied him. 'Okay, now separate them into pairs and start crossing them over.'

Hal tried, but the lines tangled up worse than ever. Instead of a bowstring, he ended up with a plate of spaghetti. Mmm. Spaghetti.

Spearman laughed. 'Was that a peal of thunder?'

'No, it was my stomach.'

'Try not to think about food.' Spearman took the hunting knife and cut a deep notch in the log, then trapped one end of his string in the V. 'You work on this one, and I'll try and sort yours out.'

Hal crouched by the log and started plaiting the bowstring, hand over hand. It didn't look very straight, but he figured the bow would soon take care of that.

Meanwhile Spearman dealt with Hal's first effort, picking at the jumbled ball of fishing wire until he'd separated the strands. By the time he'd finished Hal was at the end of his own bowstring, and he held the loose threads until Spearman could tie it off.

Stinky did really well with the bowstring, working quickly and accurately. Hal's was a bit rougher, with a couple of knots and one spot where he'd looped the line back on itself.

'Not bad,' said Spearman, as he inspected the result in the firelight. 'Good job.'

Hal felt a rush of pride.

Next, Spearman took one of the notched poles and hooked the bowstring over one end. He stood up and turned the pole over, sticking the tied end into the ground just outside his left foot. He stepped over the pole with his right foot, and the wood creaked as he bent it forward, pressing it against the back of his leg. It bent further and further until Hal thought it was going to snap, but Spearman slipped the loose end of the bowstring over the tip. When he was done the pole was bent into a curve, and the plaited string was stretched tight. Hal was impressed, and he resolved to smuggle some wooden poles aboard the Space Station when they eventually went home. Maybe they could hold an archery tournament in the recycling centre!

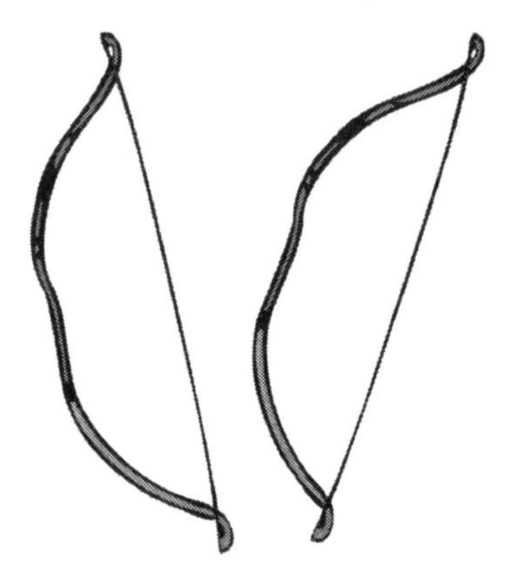

Spearman plucked the string, which made a deep twang. Then he strung a second bow using the spare string.

'What about arrows?' asked Hal, who'd just realised they had nothing to shoot.

'Try and find some straight sticks, about as thick as your little finger.'

Hal dug through the pile of firewood with gusto, tossing aside branches and snapping off anything that might make a decent arrow. When he was finished he had about two dozen sticks, and he carried them back to the fire.

Spearman took the bundle and held them over the flames, turning them whenever they started smouldering. Then he reversed them to harden the other end, holding the hot sticks with a rag. When he was happy, he took up the hunting knife and sharpened the sticks to a point. 'We need vanes to make them fly properly. I don't suppose you saw any feathers when you were gathering wood?'

Hal shook his head.

'Never mind. I'll use wrappers from the ration bars.'

Hal watched, fascinated, as Spearman cut triangles from the plastic wrappers. Then the pilot split the blunt end of the arrows, cutting a slot six or seven centimetres deep, before sliding the triangle inside. Finally, he tied around the split end with some fishing line, tying it off neatly.

'Want to try it?' he asked, offering Hal one of the bows.

Did he ever! Hal took the bow and tested the string, pulling it back to his ear. He let go and the bow went twannggg!

'Don't fire it without an arrow,' said Spearman. 'The shock will destroy the wood.'

'Sorry. I didn't know.'

Spearman passed him the arrow and showed him how to fit it to the bow. When he was ready, Hal pulled back on the string until his muscles creaked, aimed at a tree and . . . twannggg! The arrow sped into the darkness.

Thunk!

'Good shot!' said Spearman.

Hal beamed. His first go with a bow and arrow, and he'd hit the target! He fetched the arrow, which was lying on the ground next to the thick tree trunk. Of course, animals were a lot smaller than trees, so they'd be much harder to hit. And truth be told, he didn't like the idea of killing anything. He decided he'd practice with the bow as much as possible, but he wouldn't shoot creatures unless he was desperate for food.

Kent Spearman seemed to read his thoughts. 'We'll follow that stream tomorrow and see if it turns into something bigger. If so, you can hunt fish with the bow and arrow.'

Hal brightened. Fish were different somehow, and they were getting short of food. He sat on the log and watched Spearman making arrows, and all of a sudden he yawned. It was getting late, and the warmth of the fire was sending him to sleep.

'You two kip inside the capsule,' said Spearman. 'I'll sit here and keep the fire going for a bit.'

The boys didn't argue. They crawled inside and settled on two of the couches with a blanket each. Firelight played on the walls, and the crackling flames lulled them to sleep in no time.

— 15 —

Hunting

Captain Spacejock checked his weapons one last time. They'd landed in darkness, hoping to take the pirates by surprise, and every member of his team was under strict orders: no noise! They were outnumbered, outgunned, and if they tipped their foes off too soon . . . they'd lose the battle for sure.

Bzzzz-glglglgl!

Hal woke with a start, and for a second or two he thought he was in his bunk aboard Space Station Oberon. From the sound of it, someone was in his cabin, making holes in the wall with a very loud hammer drill.

Bzzzz-glglglgl!

It was very dark, but a small amount of light came through a door near his feet. Then it all came back: the damaged passenger ship, the escape pod, and the wild flight through space.

Bzzzz-glglglgl!

What *was* that noise? It sounded like wild boars, or hunting dogs, or maybe a whole gang of angry bunny rabbits. Did rabbits roar? Hal wasn't sure, but whatever it was, it sounded pretty angry.

Bzzzz . . . glglglgl.

Hal peered across the capsule and saw Kent Spearman lying on the bunk opposite. The pilot was fast asleep, and his snoring was loud enough to wake the dead.

Bzzzz . . . glglglgl.

Hal threw off his blanket and hopped down onto the floor. He was very hungry, but he had a brilliant idea: They'd find the river, catch some fish and get breakfast cooking before Mr Spearman woke up! Hal put his shoes on, then shook Stinky out of his sleep.

'Wassat? Whoozat? Where am I?' Stinky rubbed his eyes. 'What time is it?'

'Breakfast time. Come on.'

Bzzzz . . . glglglgl.

'Who's drilling holes in the wall with a hammer drill?'

Hal nodded towards Kent Spearman.

'Oh.' Stinky got up, and together they crawled out of the pod via the trench. The forest was very still and cold, and there was a light mist between the trees. The campfire was almost out, but Hal managed to get it going again with a handful of leaves and sticks. The flames were barely visible in daylight, but there was plenty of smoke.

'You mentioned breakfast?' said Stinky, looking around hopefully.

'Sure. We just have to catch it.'

Stinky groaned. 'Hal, I was dreaming about eggs and bacon!'

'You can't eat dreams. Come on, grab a bow.'

They went to collect the weapons Spearman had made the night before, but they discovered the pilot had unstrung them. Instead of the fearsome bows Hal was expecting, they were just wooden poles with a knotted string tied to one end.

Stinky picked one up and swished it back and forth. 'Maybe we could tie a hook on the string and go fishing?'

'What are you going to use for bait? Ear wax?'

'No, big green bogies!'

They both laughed. Then their stomachs rumbled. 'You look for hooks and I'll get the bows set up. Maybe the fish will bite on chunks of food ration.'

While Stinky went to look in the emergency kit, Hal inspected the bows. Spearman had unhooked the strings and Hal wasn't sure how to put them back again. He tried bending one around a tree but it didn't work: he needed two hands to bend the bow and another to fit the string. Then he remembered how Mr Spearman had stepped over the bow and bent it across the back of his leg. Hal tried it, but the wooden pole tripped him over and he fell headlong into the dirt. He brushed himself down and tried again, straining the wood until he got the string near the end, but he wasn't strong enough to bend it all the way.

Stinky came back with a small tin. 'I found some hooks, and there's a packet of dried bait.'

'Good.'

'Mr Spearman was waking up, so I told him we were going fishing. He said we should try not to drown.'

'Okay, give me a hand getting this string back on.' Hal bent the pole around a tree, straining and puffing, and Stinky attached the plaited bowstring. Then they spotted a small problem: they'd strung the bow with the tree in the middle, and there was no way to get it off. Muttering under his breath, Hal bent the pole again while Stinky removed the string . . . again.

'Forget the bow,' said Stinky. 'We'll fish instead.'

'I'm not going without a bow,' said Hal stubbornly. He looked around for inspiration and saw two big logs nearby. He laid the pole across them and got

Stinky to sit on it. The bow bent all the way to the ground and Hal had no trouble hooking the string on. He raised the bow and twanged it a couple of times, pretending to shoot wild bears and space monsters.

'Mr Spearman said not to fire it without an arrow.'

'I wasn't firing it, I was checking the string.' Hal looked around and saw the arrows leaning against the escape pod. He took half, then slung the bow over his shoulder and led Stinky down the hill. His stomach was grumbling, and when he found the stream he stopped for a good long drink. Suitably refreshed, he decided to follow the running water downhill.

As they picked their way down the valley, jumping rocks and pushing through the undergrowth, Hal wished the rest of their class could be there to share the adventure. This was *real* camping: surviving in the wild, not sitting around in brightly-coloured tents in the corner of a park! He just wished they had something to eat.

— 16 —

Fish food

The stream got bigger the further it went downhill, then vanished into the undergrowth. Hal barged through the bushes and stopped. He'd almost fallen headlong into the river.

The river was five or ten metres wide, and Hal could see the bottom through the sparkling clear water. He saw a shadow, and when he looked closer he made out the outline of a fish. Was it really going to be that easy? Hal nocked an arrow, drew back and . . . Twanng! Splash!

The fish darted off, and Hal saw the arrow slowly floating away. That's when he remembered the important thing about fishing with a bow: you had to tie your arrow to the fishing line.

Oh well, he still had five arrows.

Stinky handed him the fishing reel, and Hal took the loose end and tied it around an arrow with one of his special patented knots. By the time he finished, half the reel was knotted around the arrow, which now weighed twice as much as before.

Stinky laughed at the sight. 'If you don't hit anything with the pointy end you can always use it as a club.'

Hal ignored him and fitted the arrow to the bowstring. He drew the bow back and peered into the river, looking for fish. The big one had vanished, but there were several smaller ones swimming around in the shallows. He took aim, then released the arrow.

Twanng! SPLASH!

The fish scattered, and the arrow bobbed on the surface of the water. Hal retrieved it hand over hand, muttering under his breath. Why couldn't the fish stay still?

'Maybe we could throw stones at them,' said Stinky.

'Maybe I could throw you at them,' growled Hal. The arrow was soaking wet, and the big ball of twine on the end now weighed as much as a brick. He was beginning to think fishing with arrows was impossible, and he'd have given anything for a stale ration bar. Still, he wasn't one to give up, so he drew the arrow back and waited for the fish to settle.

'You need to aim below them,' said Stinky. 'Do you remember Teacher's lesson on refraction?'

Hal never remembered any of Teacher's lessons, especially maths. 'How are fractions going to help me catch fish?'

'Not fractions . . . refractions,' said Stinky. 'Light bends when you shine it through water.'

'Don't be a feeb. I'm not shining anything, am I?'

Stinky rolled his eyes. 'Listen, when light travels through water it slows down, and that makes things look bigger than they really are. It even makes them look like they're in a different place.'

'Don't be silly. It's just water, not some magical liquid.'

'Try it. Hold the end of the arrow in the water.'

Hal did so, and nearly fell in. The straight piece of wood looked like it had a sharp bend! He swished it around and tried moving it in and out of the water.

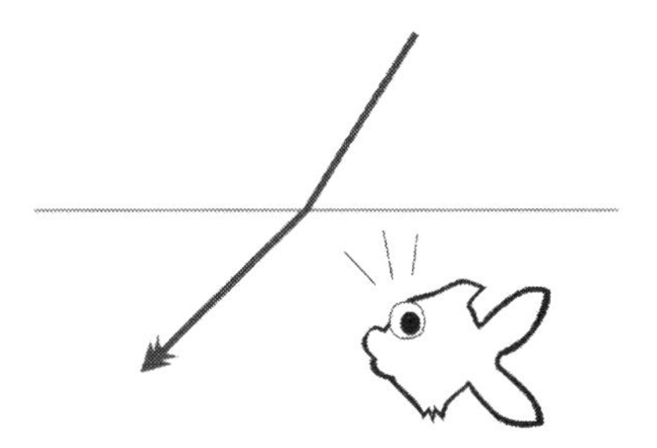

'You see? When you were shooting at the fish you were aiming over their heads. That's why you kept missing.'

‘You could have mentioned this fraction stuff before I wasted an arrow,’ grumbled Hal. ‘That big fish would have made a great breakfast.’

‘I’m sure there are plenty more.’

‘Not here there aren’t. They took one look at the arrow and cleared off.’

‘I don’t think they’d have recognised it.’

Hal pointed at the water. ‘Do you see any fish?’

‘No,’ admitted Stinky.

‘Right then. Now what?’

‘We should think of it like a chess game.’

‘You mean we should make swords, like knights, and chop the fish up?’

‘No, nothing like that. Teacher says you have to think like your opponent, and then you’ll know how to defeat them. Put yourself in your enemy’s shoes.’

‘Did Teacher mention fish don’t have shoes?’

Stinky ignored him. He thought for a moment then opened his eyes wide, made his mouth into a big O, and starting opening and closing it. Next he walked around in circles, weaving his head from side to side and waving his hands like fins.

‘It’s okay, you can stop now,’ said Hal.

‘You mean you know how to catch the fish?’ said Stinky hopefully.

‘No need. They all died laughing.’

'This is serious, Hal! Unless we think like a fish . . .'

'You don't need to think like a fish!' said Hal. 'What would you do if someone fired arrows at you?'

'Hide behind a tree.'

'Exactly.' Hal pointed down-river, where a dead tree was lying in the shallows. The thick trunk was halfway out of the water, and the tip of the longest branch almost reached the opposite bank. 'There's bound to be fish hiding underneath.'

They made their way along the bank, fighting the thick undergrowth. They had to cross several streams, and their shoes were heavy with mud by the time they reached the fallen tree. Roots stuck into the air like splayed fingers, and there was a big hole where they'd been buried in the ground. Hal bent a root back so he could get past, then released it.

Thwack!

'Ow!' shouted Stinky. 'Do you mind?'

The root had flicked back and caught him across the chest, almost knocking him off his feet. Worse, the blow had knocked the metal tin out of his hand, and the contents were scattered all over the ground. They found the fishing line and bait easily enough, but could only find two hooks.

'How many were there?' asked Hal.

‘Lots more than that,’ said Stinky. He peered in the tin. ‘Mr Spearman won’t be happy.’

‘He’ll be fine if we take some fish back.’

— 17 —

Eddy's in the river

When they got to the tree, they discovered it was covered in slippery green moss. Stinky favoured fishing from the safety of the bank, but Hal wasn't having that. He stepped onto the log, holding the bow out like a balancing pole. He'd only taken two steps when he froze.

'What is it?' demanded Stinky. 'Is it a really big fish?'

Hal shook his head. He'd spotted something far more interesting: there was a little wooden boat tied up in the shelter of the log. It was half-filled with leaves and water, but imagine if they could empty it out! They could follow the fish wherever they went . . . maybe even cross the river!

Hal heard Stinky gasp. His friend had climbed onto the log, and was staring at the little rowing boat as though it were an alien battlecruiser. 'Hal, do you know what this means?'

'No more walking.'

'Well yes, but it also means people. Civilisation. Food!'

Hal looked doubtful. The boat had plants growing inside it, and it looked very old. For all he knew it might have a big hole in the bottom. 'We need something to empty it out. And we'll need a couple of poles to push it along with.'

'We need oars,' said Stinky.

'Those too.'

They both looked around hopefully, but there were no oars to be seen.

'Maybe they're inside the boat, under that mucky water,' said Stinky.

Neither of them made a move. The water inside the boat was green and murky, and for all they knew there could be water snakes or vicious crabs or rats or slimy wriggly creatures living under the surface. Crocodiles, even, if they were little ones.

'We could tip it over,' suggested Hal.

'Let's see whether the boat is sitting on the bottom. If there's a big hole in it, we can forget about using it.'

They stumbled down the steep bank to the river, slipping and sliding in the mud. Hal pulled his shoes off, rolled up his trousers and waded into the water. He winced as the mud squidged between his toes, and he was worried the water might get deeper and deeper. Fortunately it only came up to his knees before levelling off. He put one hand on the wooden boat and tried rocking it. It moved sluggishly, but was definitely afloat.

'Try pulling it closer to the shore,' said Stinky, who was hovering on the bank like a mother duck watching her babies.

Hal grabbed hold of the rope and pulled on it to find out what it was tied to. To his surprise he came up with a loose, ragged end. 'It's not tied to anything. Why didn't it float away?'

'It must be eddies,' said Stinky.

Hal frowned. 'How do you know who it belongs to?'

'It's the swirls in the water.' Stinky pointed at the river. 'It flows past the trunk and some of it comes around here and moves backwards. That's why the boat got stuck here.'

'Do you think Eddy will mind if we borrow it?'

'Who's Eddy?'

'You said this was Eddy's boat.'

'I didn't!'

'Yes you did. You said it was Eddy's, and he was keeping it here.'

Stinky laughed. 'I didn't say it was Eddy's boat, I said it was trapped by the eddies in the river.'

'So now it's his river too? Does this Eddy guy own everything?'

'Oh, for goodness sake!' Stinky pointed with both hands. 'Look, will you? Eddies in the river!'

Hal stared, expecting to see the mysterious Eddy swimming around in a pair of trunks. All he could see was the big fallen tree and a whole lot of water. 'Where is he, then?'

'Swirls, Hal. Whirlpools.' Stinky pointed again. 'Look, those ripples. They're called eddies.'

'Why didn't you say that instead of using someone's name?' demanded Hal bitterly. 'Here I was thinking Eddy was going to tell me off for messing with his boat.'

'Teacher explained all about eddies. Remember that lesson . . . ' Stinky paused. 'All right, forget about eddie.'

'About time,' grumbled Hal. 'And if you see Tom or Dick in the river, keep them to yourself too.'

Stinky muttered under his breath, but Hal ignored him. He managed to drag the boat to the bank, where Stinky took the rope gingerly between finger and thumb. 'It's not going to bite you,' said Hal.

'No, but it's dirty.'

Hal saw red at this. He'd been wading around in the freezing cold river, getting muddy and wet while Stinky rabbited on about Invisible Eddy and his magical whirlpools. Now that he'd rescued the boat all by himself, Stinky was too fussy to grab a wet rope? 'If you don't hold it properly I'll dunk your head in the mud.'

Stinky held the rope properly, while Hal peered into the murky water. 'I can see something on the bottom. And,' he said, before Stinky could speak, 'it is not Eddy or any of his friends.'

'Is it a pair of oars?'

'No. It looks like a tin.' Hal rolled his sleeve up and reached into the water, pulling a face at the nasty rotting smell. His fingers closed on a small tin, and he pulled it out for a closer look. It was a tin can, still sealed, but the label had long since disappeared.

'What do you think is inside?'

'I don't know, but I bet it belongs to Eddy,' muttered Hal.

'It might be food. Is there an expiry date?'

Hal turned the can over and saw a grey touchpad on the bottom. Underneath the pad there was a tick and a cross. He touched the pad, and the tick turned green. 'Hey, it's still okay!'

Stinky eyed the can doubtfully. 'I bet it isn't. It's been sitting in that slime for years. Anyway, you don't know for sure that it's food.'

Hal looked into the water, hoping to spot the label floating around. Instead, he saw another can. This one was bigger, but when he fished it out he discovered it was empty. He was about to throw it away when Stinky stopped him.

'No, wait,' he said. 'We can use that for a bailer.'

Hal's eyes narrowed. 'Is Bailer another of your imaginary friends?'

'No, a bailer is used to scoop the water out of a boat.'

'Like this, you mean?' Hal dipped the can in the water and tipped the contents over the side. It didn't move much water, but as he continued, the level started to drop little by little. Within a few minutes the water was low enough to see a dozen tin cans and a metal box. Hal reached for the box, then drew back in alarm as a large frog leapt from the water and sat on top of it. Hal stared at the frog, fascinated. The frog stared right back.

'I don't think they bite,' said Stinky doubtfully.

Hal wasn't so sure. The frog had a pretty big mouth, and there was plenty of room for two rows of fearsome teeth. He'd seen a movie once where things like this leaped across rooms to attack their prey. And here he was, face to face with it.

All of a sudden the frog puffed out its cheeks, and . . . *Ribbit!*

Startled, Hal stepped back, losing his balance and sitting down in the squidgy mud.

Ribbit ribbit! went the frog.

'I think it's laughing at you,' said Stinky.

Hal leapt up, dripping mud. The frog didn't sound very dangerous, and he wondered whether he could put it in his pocket and smuggle it back to the Space Station. But no, it looked like it lived in water, and that was something they were very short of at home. 'Go on, shoo!' he said, flapping his hands at it.

The frog gave him a disgusted look and sprang into the river, landing with a plop and a splash.

Hal wasted no time. He took hold of the box, snapped the catches and opened the lid. Water poured out, and then inside he saw . . . a chrome-plated blaster! It had a checkered black hand grip and a long slender barrel, and it was the most amazing thing Hal had ever seen.

'Is that real?' asked Stinky.

'I bet it is.' Hal reached into the box for the gun, then stopped. Guns were dangerous at the best of times, and this one had been underwater for years. Imagine if it went off when he touched it? Or imagine if the charge pack exploded? Carefully he closed the lid, and then he tucked the box under the big tree. 'We'll tell Mr Spearman about it. He'll know what to do.'

Stinky nodded.

'Come on, help me get the other tins out.'

The boys tipped the boat to remove the last of the water, then plucked the tins from the goopy green mess in the bottom. There were fourteen of them, all different shapes and sizes, and not one of them had a label. Hal and Stinky used the freshness tester on each, and they ended up with nine good tins and five which had gone bad.

'We should take them back to Mr Spearman,' said Stinky. 'He'll be getting worried, and he's probably twice as hungry as we are.'

Hal eyed the boat. He really wanted to try it out, but Stinky was right. They would take the food to the capsule, have breakfast and come back afterwards. He grabbed some leaves and covered the tin box with the gun inside, and then he and Stinky set off back to camp.

— 18 —

Hot food

When they arrived at the escape pod there were no signs of life. Stinky went inside to get Kent, but he re-appeared in the doorway immediately. 'He's not here.'

'Don't be daft. He must be.'

'Check for yourself.'

Hal crawled through the tunnel and stood up. After the bright daylight, it was dark inside the capsule, and he felt his way around carefully. There were blankets, and a pair of shoes, but there was definitely no Kent Spearman. After a few minutes his eyes adjusted, and he could see at a glance that the capsule was empty. 'He can't have gone far, not with a bad ankle.'

'Maybe it got better.'

'Not that quickly.' Hal had twisted his ankle once, and afterwards it was several days before he could put weight on it.

'Hal . . . you don't think he went looking for us?'

'Even Captain Spacejock wouldn't trek around the forest with an injury like that.'

'But if he did . . . do you think he left a message?'

'A secret message?' Hal looked hopeful. 'In code?'

They searched the pod, but apart from the blankets all they found were a couple of empty storage compartments. 'Let's check outside,' said Hal. 'He might have pinned a note to a tree with his hunting knife. Maybe he wrote something in the blood of his enemies.'

'There aren't any enemies.'

'Oh yeah? What if he's been captured?'

'If he was captured, he wouldn't have time to run around pinning notes to trees, would he?'

Hal thought for a moment. 'He might have scratched a message in the dirt.'

They spent five minutes scouring the area around the pod, but all they found were lots of footprints - mostly their own. Hal did find something which could have sort have been a message, if you looked at it sideways, until Stinky pointed out it was caused by a branch they'd dragged to the fire the night before.

'What next?' asked Stinky.

It was approaching lunchtime and they hadn't

even had breakfast yet. Back on the Space Station he'd dreamed about camping in the woods: sleeping in a snug tent, cooking eggs and bacon and swimming in the river. Instead he'd spent an uncomfortable night in the capsule, he'd had nothing to eat and the river had been freezing cold and teeming with dangerous frogs and skittish fish. At that moment, if someone offered to wave a magic wand and transport him back to Space Station Oberon he'd have been sorely tempted. If only he wasn't so hungry! 'I know. Let's try one of the cans.'

'It might be off.'

'We'll sniff it first. If it smells okay we'll try a tiny bit each, and then we'll wait an hour or two. If we feel all right, we'll eat the rest of the tin.'

'That's pretty good thinking.'

'No need to look so surprised.' Hal returned to the pod and selected the biggest tin. He pressed down in the middle of the lid and turned his thumb sideways, and the can opened with a hiss. Inside there were half a dozen cylinders, all vacuum sealed in foil.

'What are they?' asked Stinky. 'Biscuits? Cheese sticks? Cured sausages?'

'No,' said Hal, who'd just finished reading the label. 'They're battery packs for that pistol.'

Stinky started to back way. 'Do you . . . do you think the rest might be hand grenades?'

Hal went pale as he remembered the rough way they'd handled the tins. They'd had to carry five or six each, and they'd dropped them all several times on the way back. They could have set off a huge explosion! Then he relaxed. If dropping them hadn't blown them up, opening them would be safe enough. 'Hide behind a tree if you like. One of them might have food in, and I'm going to find it.'

Stinky hesitated, then came back. 'I'll do the next one.' He examined the tins, then picked a small square one. The lid was dented where Hal had dropped it on a rock, but it popped open with a hiss under Stinky's thumb. Inside were two slabs of brown . . . plasticine?

'Great. Now we can make zoo animals,' said Hal.

'It might be food.' Stinky sniffed the pale brown slabs, then coughed and wrinkled his nose in distaste. 'No,' he wheezed. 'Not food. Chemicals of some kind.'

Hal picked up a flat tin with rounded corners. Hiss! went the lid, and he peered inside hopefully. Success! There was a thick stew with a spoon in, and he had to put the can down quickly as it became too hot to hold. The heating element warmed the food up in seconds, and Hal's stomach growled at the delicious smell.

'Remember, it might be off,' said Stinky.

Hal breathed deeply, and his mouth watered. 'If that's off I'm a teacher's pet,' he declared.

'One spoonful each. That was the rule.'

'But then it'll get cold!'

'Just one spoonful, then we wait.'

'Who put you in charge?' grumbled Hal. He plucked the spoon out of the stew and scooped up as much as he could, then shovelled it into his mouth. The taste was heavenly, and it was all he could do not to gulp it down. Instead, he passed the spoon to Stinky and chewed on the mouthful for as long as possible, enjoying the rich meat and vegetable flavours to the very last drop.

Stinky took a mouthful and chewed in silence, his face a study of concentration. Gulp! The food was gone, and he sighed. 'Now we have to wait an hour.'

Hal looked at Stinky. Stinky looked at Hal. They both looked at the tin.

'It was a silly rule anyway,' said Hal, and he

reached for the spoon.

The can of stew lasted two minutes, and they each got half a dozen mouthfuls of delicious food. It was very tasty, but they were both still hungry and they longed for more. There were only a few tins left, though, and they couldn't afford to open another.

After a few minutes of silence, Hal filled the empty tin from the stream. They both drank deeply, draining every last drop. 'That's breakfast dealt with,' said Hal at last. 'Now let's find Kent Spearman.'

— 19 —

Meeting

They climbed to the top of the hill, hoping it would give them a better view of the surroundings. Unfortunately, all they could see was trees.

'Maybe we should wait for him near the pod,' said Stinky.

'What if his ankle got worse?' Hal gestured down the other side of the hill. 'He could be stuck out there somewhere.'

'We should never have left this morning. Not without telling him where we were going.'

'We didn't know where we were going,' said Hal shortly. He wasn't a big fan of 'we should have' and 'we ought to have'. What was done, was done.

'Maybe we could try whistling.'

Hal frowned. Out of the entire class, he was the only one who hadn't mastered the really loud whistle Teacher had tried to show them all. He suspected Stinky had only suggested whistling so he could show his own off. Then his face cleared. 'Of course! He's gone hunting!'

'Do you think so?'

'I bet he has. He probably made another bow and arrows, and set off to get dinner.' Hal realised something. 'If he's hunting we'd better not make a sound. We'll scare the game away.'

'What are we going to do, then?'

Hal thought for a moment. 'Okay, we'll go down the other side of the hill then circle round. He can't be far away, and he might see us.'

'He might shoot us,' said Stinky in alarm.

'Do I look like a rabbit to you?'

Stinky looked him up and down. 'I guess not,' he said doubtfully.

'Right. Follow me, then.'

They made their way down the steep slope, pushing through the undergrowth and keeping an eye out for Kent Spearman. At the bottom of the hill they turned left, and after half an hour they heard something totally unexpected: voices!

'Do you hear them?' whispered Hal.

'Of course,' Stinky whispered back. 'And Hal . . . '

'Yes?'

'Why are we whispering?'

'We don't know who it is, do we?'

'Maybe Mr Spearman found help.'

'Yeah, and maybe it's those fugitives from the news flash.'

'The bank robbers?' Stinky gulped, then realised Hal was leaving. 'Hey, where are you going?'

'To get a better look.' Hal crawled under a bush, parted the branches and peered between the leaves. He imagined he was Captain Spacejock tracking a deadly enemy, and he was disappointed to see two ordinary-looking adults sitting on tree stumps near a blazing campfire. They were wearing dark clothing, and had broad webbed belts with knives and pouches. Hal realised they weren't fugitives or bank robbers . . . they were hunters! The man had red hair and a freckled face, while the woman was darker with short black hair. Then Hal sniffed. There was a pot hanging over the fire, and the contents smelled delicious. His spirits rose. Not only had they found help, they might get lunch too!

'It's going to be another cold night,' said the woman.

'I hate these woods,' said the man. 'They give me the creeps.'

'That's because you're scared of your own shadow.' She laughed. 'If someone leapt out of the bushes right now –'

'Excuse me,' said Hal loudly.

The adults jumped, springing to their feet. They stared into the bushes, directly towards the boys' hiding place. 'Who is it?' demanded one. 'Show yourself!'

Hal set the bow and arrows down and crawled out of the bush.

'It's just a kid,' said the woman.

'There are two of us,' said Hal, as Stinky appeared at his side. 'Our ship fell apart, and we crashed last night. We . . . we don't have any food.'

'You look all in, the pair of you,' said the man kindly. He had a good-humoured face with lots of freckles, and Hal warmed to him straight away. 'Here, come and sit down. There's plenty of hot grub to go around.'

The boys didn't need to be asked twice. They sat on the tree stump, took bowls of stew and wolfed them down.

The man tapped himself in the chest. 'I'm Ted and this is Amber. And you are?'

'I'm Hal, and this is Stink–, er, Stephen.'

'Nice to meet you both.' Ted hesitated. 'So, are you out here alone?'

Stinky shook his head. 'Mr Spearman is back at the escape pod. He hurt his ankle during the landing.'

'Sounds like you had a lucky escape.'

With the food now warming his stomach, Hal turned his mind to other matters. 'You're hunters, aren't you? Have you caught anything yet?'

Amber laughed. 'Hunters. Yes, that's us.'

Hal looked around curiously. 'Where are you staying? Do you have a tent?'

'More of a shelter. We came out here a week ago in a neat little flyer, but this dummy left the lights on.' Amber slapped Ted on the shoulder. 'The battery went flat, and now we can't open the ship. Isn't that a laugh?' Despite her words, she looked a long way from laughter. In fact, she looked seriously annoyed.

'You had to bring that up again, didn't you?' Now Ted sounded angry. 'I already told you –'

'Lucky for him,' interrupted Amber, speaking to Hal, 'we got the gear out of the ship first.'

'So it's just the two of you?' asked Hal.

'That's right. Me and my best buddy Ted.'

‘Don’t you have enough power to radio for help?’ asked Hal. ‘I think Mr Spearman needs a doctor.’

Ted shook his head. ‘No radio. We can make a splint though, maybe get him comfortable.’

‘I have an idea,’ said Stinky.

Everyone turned to look at him.

‘I–I was just thinking, we might be able to take batteries from the capsule and use them to power up your ship.’

‘Aren’t you the bright one?’ said Amber, with a tight smile.

‘They’ll be heavy, but we could manage with a travois.’

Hal frowned. Was Travis another one of Stinky’s imaginary friends?

‘Mr Spearman is good with ships, and I know a thing or two about electronics,’ added Stinky. ‘Between us I’m sure we could rig something up.’

‘This Spearman. Is he your teacher?’

‘No, he’s the pilot.’

The adults exchanged a glance. ‘Pilot, eh? That’s handy.’

Hal liked the sound of the plan. They could find Mr Spearman, get the batteries, fix the hunters’ ship and call for help. ‘Hey, maybe we could fly out of here,’ he said suddenly.

‘Sounds perfect to me,’ said Ted. ‘What do you think, Amber?’

‘One hundred percent agreement,’ said Amber. ‘Let’s go talk to Mr Spearman.’

— 20 —

Travis

When they reached the pod there was still no sign of Kent Spearman. Amber glanced inside, then frowned at Hal and Stinky. 'So where's this pilot of yours?'

'We think he went hunting,' said Hal.

Ted and Amber exchanged a glance. 'He has a gun?'

'No, we made bows and arrows out of sticks and fishing line.'

Amber nodded, and immediately started giving orders. 'Take the cushions off the seats, rip lengths of wire from the pod's console, and if you can loosen any wall panels grab those too. You never know what we might need.'

While Ted and the boys stripped everything of use from the capsule, Amber took the axe and chopped down a couple of small trees. She stripped the branches with half a dozen strokes, then lashed the narrow ends together to make a large 'A'. When it was ready she laid a blanket on top and called for the equipment, which she piled in the middle. 'Anything else?'

Ted held up a shovel. 'I found this in a compartment under the seat.'

'Good. That could be useful.'

Once everything was sitting on the blanket, Amber wrapped it up and tied it to the poles with lengths of wire. She tested the weight, and nodded. 'It's heavy, but we'll manage.'

Hal looked around the clearing. 'We should leave a note for Mr Spearman, telling him where we are.'

Ted and Amber exchanged a glance. 'I'll do it,' said Amber. 'You go ahead.'

Ted stood between the poles, holding one in each hand like a wheelbarrow in reverse. Hal and Stinky stood in front of him, holding one end each. On the count of three they all lifted together and staggered forwards. The travois bumped and scraped over the rough ground, and Hal couldn't help being impressed. The pole was rough on his hand, but the load was manageable. It would have been a lot worse if they'd had to carry everything.

It was a good hour before they arrived at the hunters' ship. It was a sleek grey flyer with swept-back wings, and Hal could see two seats inside, one behind the other. One wing had green branches over it, woven together to form an A-shaped shelter. Underneath the body of the flyer, on the ground, he could see a small pile of supplies: tinned food, a plastic drum of water and a couple of crates.

They set the travois down carefully, and Hal and Stinky flexed their hands and shoulders to ease the aches and pains. Ted had a quick drink before unpacking the salvaged equipment, dividing it up into piles. 'We'll build you a shelter under the other wing,' he said. 'Can you fetch some branches? Those trees with the big leaves are best.'

Hal and Stinky headed into the woods, where they spent twenty minutes pulling green leafy branches from the trees. Hal was careful to break the branches off cleanly, instead of pulling them down and tearing great strips of bark from the trunk. They'd taught him that in the hydroponics lab aboard the Space Station, explaining that the branches would eventually regrow that way.

They ended up with armfuls of bushy branches, which they dragged back to the clearing. Ted selected the three largest and propped the splintered ends against the flyer's wing. Then he showed the boys how to weave and twist smaller branches between them, filling the gaps to block out cold wind and - hopefully - any rain.

After several hours, and many more trips to fetch branches, the new shelter was finally ready. There were two leafy green walls, one on either side of the wing, and the entrance was finished off with a blanket from the escape pod. Inside was snug, like a living tent, and Hal couldn't wait to try it out at night.

He clambered outside again and found Ted inspecting a pile of equipment from the escape pod. 'You should get Stinky to look at those batteries. He might be able to wire them into your ship so you can call for help.'

Ted smiled. 'I'm sure you're both very clever, but I'm not risking things getting even worse.'

'Stinky wouldn't make things worse. He'd have that thing going in no time.'

'No, it'll be dark soon. We'll take another look in the morning.'

⬥

It was late at night, and Hal was snug and warm inside his blankets. Stinky was nearby, fast asleep and snoring gently. They'd enjoyed a dinner of hot stew, and afterwards Ted told them funny stories about his childhood. Amber barely spoke a word all evening, just sitting and gazing into the fire.

After one particularly hair-raising tale involving a jetbike, a length of rope and an old wooden crate, Stinky had given a huge yawn. Not long after, Ted had sent the boys to their tent. He and Amber stayed up, tending the fire.

Hal gazed up at the underside of the flyer's metal wing, wondering what might have happened to Kent Spearman. He hadn't shown up yet, and Hal hoped the blanket and food they'd left at the capsule would keep the pilot going until the morning. Hal wondered where he'd got to, especially with his injured ankle. He felt they could have done more to search for the missing pilot, but night had closed in quickly and they might have ended up with two or three people missing instead of just one.

Moments later his eyes closed, and he drifted off to sleep.

Hal woke with a start. He wasn't sure how long he'd been asleep, and as the fog in his brain cleared he realised he could hear raised voices. In the next shelter, on the other side of the flyer, Ted and Amber were arguing about something. Hal strained his ears, trying to pick out a word or two, but their voices were muffled.

He lay there in the blankets, snug and warm. Hal knew their argument was none of his business, but he suspected they might be arguing about him and Stinky, or about the search for Kent Spearman. They were probably saying things they didn't want Hal to hear, but that made him even keener to hear them.

Unfortunately it was dark, it was very cold, and the last thing he wanted to do was sneak around in the bushes listening to private conversations.

'They know too much, that's all I'm saying.'

Amber's voice was loud, and no sooner had she spoken than Hal heard Ted's reply.

'They're just kids, Amber. What can they do?'

'Plenty, if they talk to the wrong people.'

'They swallowed the hunters story, didn't they?'

'Yeah, they believed it. Their pilot is another matter.'

'I thought you took care of him?'

'Hopefully. I left a note telling him we were heading North.'

Hal frowned. No wonder they hadn't found

Kent Spearman. Amber had sent him the wrong way! But why? Ted and Amber weren't hunters, apparently, so who were they?

'Is the stuff still in the cockpit?' asked Ted.

'Under the seat.' Amber hesitated. 'They'll have to be dealt with, you know.'

'Relax, will you? I know a guy we can sell them to.'

'Eh?'

'The gold bars. I know a guy.'

Gold? Hal's eyes widened. These two *were* the bank robbers everyone was looking for. And he and Stinky had been hanging out with them all day!

'I'm not talking about the gold,' snapped Amber. 'I meant we'd have to take care of those kids!'

Hal was wide awake now, and despite the warm blankets he was chilled to the core. He remembered when Amber found the shovel in the escape pod, and how she'd said it would prove useful 'later'.

'You can't mean –' began Ted.

'No, of course not. We'll leave them out here when we go. We'll put some food aside, maybe get word to the authorities in a day or two.'

'After the fuss dies down, you mean.'

'Yeah. In the meantime we'll have to lie low.'

There was no reply, and Hal strained his ears for all they were worth. Why had they stopped speaking? Were they whispering? Hal peeled back the blankets, and he was just about to crawl out of the shelter when he got the shock of his life.

Someone clamped a rough, muddy hand over his mouth!

— 21 —

Midnight foray

Hal struggled to get free, until he heard a frantic whisper in his ear. 'Keep still, Hal. It's me, Kent Spearman! I'm going to take my hand away, but don't make a noise. Understood?'

Hal nodded, and Kent removed his hand. 'Where have you been all day?' whispered Hal.

Kent explained quickly. He'd been hunting, as Hal had guessed, but he'd got lost on the way back. He found the pod in the end, and then he'd spotted the note.

'How did you find us here?' whispered Hal. 'I thought Amber sent you on a wild duck chase?'

'Wild goose chase,' said Kent, with a grin. 'I headed North, just like the note said, but after a couple of hours my ankle was much worse so I doubled back. It got dark, but I spotted your firelight through the trees. I crept closer to find out who it was, and then I saw you two come in here. That's when I heard the adults talking, and I realised I'd have to rescue you both. You do realise who they are, don't you?'

'Yes, they're the bank robbers from the news.'

'They might be dangerous. We have to get away from here, as far as possible, before they discover you're gone.'

'Where will we go? Back to the pod?'

Kent shook his head. 'That's the first place they'll look.'

'But your ankle. How will you get away?' Hal wondered whether he and Stinky could move Mr Spearman on the travois, but he doubted it. Anyway, Ted and Amber would catch them up in no time.

'We'll go as far as possible, and then we'll climb a tree. It's a big forest and there's a good chance we'll be able to avoid them.' Kent glanced up at the flyer. 'Unless they use this, of course.'

'They said it had a flat battery.'

'I wouldn't believe everything they told you.'

Hal thought for a moment. 'What if Stinky and I drew them away, and you started the flyer? We could meet you near the river.'

'That's not a bad idea, but I can't put you in that kind of danger. These people are desperate, and I don't like to think what might happen if they caught up with you.'

Hal shivered. Ted seemed okay but Amber was another matter. He didn't mind admitting it: she scared him. 'Hey, we left the bows and arrows under a bush. We could arm ourselves and –'

'No.' Kent shook his head. 'I'm not having either of you fighting pitched battles with these people. Is that clear?'

'I guess,' mumbled Hal. Then he remembered something. The boat! 'Mr Spearman, when Stinky and I went fishing we found something useful. There was a wooden boat next to a big tree.'

'That could be handy. Was it far?'

'No, just near the river. And . . . there was another thing.' Hal hesitated. 'There were tins of food in the bottom of the boat, as well as a metal box. We opened the box and found . . . a gun.'

Kent's eyebrows shot up. 'A what?'

'A blaster.' Hal indicated the size with his hands. 'It was about this big, and dark grey.'

'This isn't one of your games, is it?'

'No, it's true! I wanted to hunt fish with it but Stinky wouldn't let me.'

'At least one of you is sensible,' said Spearman drily. 'So what did you do with the gun?'

'I hid it under a fallen tree.'

Kent thought for a moment. 'Okay, here's what we'll do. You fetch the gun and make sure the boat is still there. Meanwhile, I'll wake Stinky and explain everything.'

Hal frowned. He thought Stinky would be coming to the boat too. He wasn't wild about tackling the woods on his own.

'One last thing,' said Kent. 'Is there any food around? I've barely eaten all day.'

'Wait here.' Hal crept under the flyer and felt around until his fingers brushed the cans of food. He grabbed two and clambered out again. When he got back to the shelter he found Stinky awake and rubbing sleep from his eyes. 'Here,' said Hal, passing Kent the tins. 'I don't know what's in them.'

'Right now I'd eat lumpy custard and raw beef . . . all mixed together.'

'Did you explain the plan to Stinky?'

'Sure did. Just one little change . . . we've decided he's going with you.'

Hal glanced at Stinky, who looked worried. He doubted Stinky had volunteered, which meant Kent had told him to go to the river with Hal . . . probably to keep an eye on him. 'It's all right, he doesn't have to come. I'll be quicker on my own.'

'I'd rather you both went,' said Kent firmly.

Hal realised this was one of those 'adult

suggestions' which were pretty much the same as direct orders. 'All right, fine.'

'Thank you. And Hal . . . '

'Yes, Mr Spearman?'

'Be careful out there.'

The boys crept out of the shelter and got to their feet. Hal had no idea how late it was, but the fire was out and the forest was silent and dark. Looking up, he could see tiny patches of night sky between the leaves and branches of the overhanging trees, and when he waved his hand in front of his face he discovered there was just enough light to see movement.

Hal turned this way and that, trying to get his bearings. He could just hear the rush and splash of moving water in the distance, and he set off in the general direction. On the way he stopped at the bush where he'd hidden with Stinky earlier that day. They dug around inside until they found the bows, grabbing as many arrows as they could find in the darkness. Mr Spearman had told him not to take the weapon, but the forest was dark and spooky. Actually, it was so dark Hal wouldn't be able to see what he was shooting at, not unless their enemies waved torches in the air and shouted 'hit me, hit me!'

With the bows slung over their shoulders and the arrows gripped in their hands, Hal and Stinky marched confidently towards the river. Five minutes later they were moving a lot more carefully: their faces and arms were scratched from low-hanging branches, and their toes hurt where they kept stubbing them on half-buried rocks.

Hal wasn't sure how far they'd come, but the river didn't seem to be getting any louder. In fact, he was starting to wonder whether they were even heading in the right direction. He would have gone back to the flyer to start again, but he wasn't sure which way that was either. Kent Spearman had used the campfire to home in on the camp, but the fire was out now.

Hal shrugged and pressed on. First they'd find the gun and the boat. Then they'd worry about getting back again.

— 22 —

Seeking

The river was a lot closer now, and there was more light filtering through the trees. Hal found a stout branch along the way, and he used it to swish a path through the leafy undergrowth. Not only did this protect his arms and face from scratches, but it also left a handy trail he could follow to get back to camp.

Swish! Crack!

'Could you make a bit more noise?' whispered Stinky. 'I think there are still a few people on this planet who don't know where we are.'

Annoyed, Hal swung the branch even harder.

Swish! CRACK!

Eventually he chopped his way through the final bushes, and they saw the river laid out in front of them. The water gleamed like polished silver in the starlight, but the far bank was like a solid black cloud. Then Hal realised something: there was no fallen tree!

Hal looked left and right, but the river was empty in both directions. Which way should he go? The escape pod had been up-river from the flyer earlier in the day, but if he'd passed it in the darkness it could be down-river now, off to his left. He was just about to head that way when Stinky spoke up.

'I think it's to our left.'

Hal frowned. Who was in charge of the expedition anyway? He was! 'Well I think it's off to the right.'

'All right, I'll go the other way.'

'I don't think we should split up,' said Hal. 'Mr Spearman said –'

'Oh, who cares what Mr Spearman said!' growled Stinky. 'He got us into this mess in the first place! If his ship hadn't broken down, if all the pods had been working, if he were a proper pilot . . . we'd be camping in proper tents with proper food instead of running around in the dark like this!'

Hal eyed his friend in surprise. He'd never known Stinky to get angry, and he wasn't sure he liked it. Stinky was calm and dependable, and if he was having a breakdown, the whole situation had to be worse than Hal thought. 'We could go left if you like.'

'I don't care which way we try first. I just want to

go home.'

'All right, follow me.' Hal was was just about to set off up-river when he remembered to mark his way. He took a fallen branch and jammed the end in the ground, creating a makeshift signpost. If he ran into that coming back again, he'd know exactly where he was.

Following the river bank sounded like an easy plan, but it was a lot tougher than they expected. Thick bushes and trees grew right down to the water's edge, which meant constant detours, and there were muddy inlets hidden under spongy moss and creepers. In the dark these looked just like any other patch of ground . . . until Hal stepped on them. Each time he did, he'd cry out in alarm as he sank right up to his knees in cold water. Stinky would help him out, and they'd make their way around the edge until they arrived at the next one . . . where Hal would promptly get another soaking.

After ten or twenty minutes they finally made it to the river bank. They were a long way up-stream, and there was no sign of the fallen tree. 'This is hopeless,' grumbled Hal. 'It's going to be light soon, and those crooks will wake up and discover we're missing.'

'It's not even midnight yet,' said Stinky.

Hal checked his impressive space watch, illuminating the big flashy screen with a flick of his wrist. He checked the time and discovered his friend was right . . . it seemed like they'd been walking for hours, but it had only been forty or fifty minutes. Hal covered his watch and stood on the river bank, deciding what to do next. They could make their way further up the river, hoping the boat would come into view. Or they could turn around and tramp all the way down-stream again. 'What do you think?' he asked Stinky.

'I think we should have turned left.'

Hal didn't bother replying. 'What if we built a raft and floated down the river? That way we wouldn't have to walk through the mud again.'

'It'll take all night to build a raft. Anyway, we don't have any logs and we certainly don't have any rope.'

Hal frowned into the darkness. The river bank was wider here, and it looked a lot easier to follow. 'Okay, we'll keep going until we hit a rough patch, and then we'll turn back.'

They walked in silence under the stars . . . silent, that is, except for the squish-squish-squish of Hal's soggy shoes. Eventually they rounded the next bend, and he squinted into the darkness. Was that a shadow on the water up ahead? 'Hey, is that the tree?'

Stinky shaded his eyes. 'I think it's more bushes.'

Hal muttered under his breath. 'Come on, we'd better check.'

They hurried forward, and as they got closer Hal's expression grew more and more hopeful. It was definitely a fallen tree, but was it the right tree? Then . . . joy! He spotted the wooden boat lying on the shore. 'That's it, Stinky. We found it!'

Hal didn't waste any time on the boat. He went straight to the fallen tree and felt underneath for the metal box. It was exactly where he'd left it, but he still held his breath as he popped the lid. If the gun wasn't there . . .

But it was, still wrapped in its protective cloth. 'Okay, give me a hand with the boat.'

Stinky looked puzzled. 'What for?'

'I'm not walking all the way back again. We'll sit in the boat and sail down the river.'

'We can't do that. We don't know how to use it!'

'Of course we do. You just get in and float along.'

'It's not that simple. We need oars to row it.'

Hal gestured at the river. 'What for? The water's already moving, isn't it?'

'How will we stop when we reach the right place?'

'We'll paddle back to shore with our hands.'

'No, I don't like it. We could get into real trouble.'

'Stinky, we survived an exploding spaceship, crash-landed in the middle of nowhere, and we're stuck in a huge forest with a wounded pilot and a pair of dangerous criminals. I'd say we're already in trouble.'

'And if the river carries us out to sea? You think we'll be better off then?'

'If that happens we'll shout for help.' Hal started to drag the boat towards the water. 'Come on, give me a hand.'

Stinky shook his head. 'It's too dangerous.'

'Fine, walk back on your own. I'll wait for you.' Hal expected Stinky to cave in, like he always did, but his friend stood firm.

'I'm not getting into that boat. You don't know what you're doing, and even if it works you'll only save a few minutes.'

'But . . . '

'No!' Stinky set off for the bushes without another word, leaving Hal alone with the boat.

'Stinky, wait!'

No reply.

'Stinky!' Hal thumped his fist on the boat. For a moment he considered pushing it onto the river anyway, heading out alone if he had to. Then he gave up and tramped into the bushes after his friend.

— 23 —

Wild animals

Hal caught up with Stinky straight away, and they made their way through the bushes together. They hadn't gone far when Hal froze. 'Did you hear that?' he whispered.

'What?'

Hal cupped his hand to his ear. 'There it was again.'

Stinky cupped *both* hands to his ears and turned his head this way and that. In the darkness he looked like a faulty radar dish, and Hal almost burst out laughing. 'I still can't hear anything,' hissed Stinky.

'Maybe it's circling round behind us.'

'Maybe *what* is?'

'I don't know. It sounded like a growl.'

Stinky turned his head even faster.

'It might have been a moan,' said Hal. 'Do bears moan in the woods, or is that wolves?'

'W-wolves?'

Hal smiled to himself. Teacher had shown them a documentary on wolves, and it had given Stinky nightmares for days. 'Oh well, it was probably nothing. Come on, time's wasting.'

Stinky didn't move. 'I think I heard it.'

'Really?' said Hal in surprise.

'I-I think maybe we should try the boat,' said Stinky.

'You said it was dangerous.'

'It's safer than a pack of wolves.'

Hal pretended to think about it. He didn't want to sound too eager in case Stinky smelled a rat . . . or a bear, or a wolf. 'All right,' he said at last. 'I agree with you. Let's take the boat instead.'

They turned tail and hurried out of the woods. When they reached the boat Hal went to push it out, but Stinky stopped him. 'Look around for a couple of branches. We can use them to fend off obstacles, and if the water isn't too deep we can pole the boat along by pushing against the riverbed.'

Hal searched the undergrowth but all he found was a short piece of stick.

'You'll want something just a bit longer than that,' said Stinky. 'It'll need to be twice your height.'

Hal roamed further afield, and he came across a fallen tree. The branches were dry and brittle, and he managed to snap two of the bigger ones off. Stinky nodded his approval, and Hal laid them in the bottom of the boat.

'Ready?' he said.

'On three,' said Stinky. 'One . . . Two . . . Three!'

They pushed the boat into the water, throwing themselves on board as it sailed away from the shore. They ended up in a heap in the bottom, and Hal made a face as his fingers encountered a layer of gooey, squishy mud. He cleaned his hands by dipping them in the water.

'I wonder if there are any sharks?' said Stinky innocently.

Hal yanked his hand out of the water.

'Then again,' said Stinky, 'your wolves and bears probably ate them all.'

The boat turned slowly as it floated down river. They were moving very slowly, and Hal decided to help it along. He grabbed one of the poles and stood up.

'Hal, sit down!' hissed Stinky, as the boat rocked like crazy. 'You'll have us over!'

Hal didn't need telling . . . he'd already sat down, and a lot harder than he meant to. He clung to the sides as the boat settled, then took the pole and tried sticking it in the water. He leant over the side, reaching down as far as he could, but the pole just moved around in the water. He opened his mouth to tell Stinky, then closed it again. Instead, he pretended to push the boat along, groaning and heaving as he struggled with the pole.

'That's working,' said Stinky. 'We're moving quicker now.'

They continued like this for several minutes, with Hal pretending to push them along. He kept his eyes on the bank, looking for the branch he'd poked into the ground. Unfortunately he could barely make out tree trunks, let alone a skinny stick. The water was bright enough, flickering and dancing with reflected starlight, but under the trees it was gloomy and dark.

'Do you want me to take a turn with that?' asked Stinky, nodding towards the pole.

'Er, no. I can manage.'

'You sound worn out.'

'It's nothing, believe me.' Hal redoubled his efforts, lifting the pole and pushing it into the water, and all the while pretending it was touching the ground.

'We're going the wrong way,' said Stinky. 'Take us closer to the shore.'

'I'm doing my best,' puffed Hal.

'Wait, I'll give you a hand.' Stinky took up the

second branch, and before Hal could stop him he stuck it in the water. He frowned, then stretched further and further until the water reached his elbow. 'Hal . . .'

'Your pole must be shorter than mine.'

'They were both the same.'

Hal gave up the deception, throwing his branch into the bottom of the boat. 'Oh, all right, I admit it. I was just pretending.'

'For how long?' demanded Stinky.

'Ever since we set off.'

Stinky opened and closed his mouth, unable to speak. Then, with big round eyes, he turned to look down-river. Hal knew exactly what his friend was thinking, because he'd already gone over it in his head. Even if they saw the marker in the darkness, they'd still float past. In fact, they could float for hours before the river washed them out to sea.

'You should have told me,' said Stinky. 'I'd have thought of something.'

'Like swimming to shore?'

'Don't be silly. Neither of us could do that.'

'What about –'

'Let me think!' snapped Stinky. He eyed the branches, then stared across at the bank, then rubbed his chin. Meanwhile, the boat continued to sail down-river. 'Okay, what we need is a longer pole.'

'Brilliant,' said Hal. 'I wish I'd thought of that.'

Stinky ignored the interruption. 'What we have is two short poles. My solution is . . . tie them together.'

Hal smiled to himself. High-tech or low-tech, Stinky always had an answer! There was just one problem. 'What about rope?'

'Shoelaces.' Stinky looked down at Hal's feet. 'They're not elastic, are they?'

'No, these are new.'

Stinky looked again. 'Er . . . is it just me, or is there a bit more water in the boat?'

'You're right. It's getting deeper.' Hal removed his shoelaces, then grabbed the big bailing tin and started emptying water over the side.

Five minutes later Stinky was ready. He'd used all four shoelaces to bind the poles together, tying the lashings off with a simple knot. Hal wanted to use one of his special knots, but the laces weren't long enough.

'Be careful with it,' said Stinky. 'It'll snap in half if you jam it into the ground.'

Hal dipped the end of the pole in the water, lowering it hand over hand. Three-quarters disappeared beneath the surface before he felt resistance. 'That's it. I can feel the river bed.'

'Try pushing us towards the shore.'

Hal did so, leaning on the pole. It bent alarmingly, but they did seem to be getting closer to the bank.

'Keep going,' said Stinky. 'It's working!'

Hal pushed again, and the boat moved. Again, and they were in the shallows. One final push and the boat grounded, heeling over as the river tried to carry it away. Hal was over the side in a flash, and he hauled the boat towards the bank. Stinky hopped out, and together they pulled it to safety.

Then Hal laughed. Five metres away, standing up from the muddy bank, was the branch he'd stuck into the ground.

— 24 —

Sail away

It was almost an hour before Hal and Stinky arrived back at camp. They were muddy and exhausted, and Hal's shoulder ached from carrying the metal tin. All the way back, he'd been wondering how they'd find the flyer in the darkness, but Kent Spearman had thought of that. He was flashing a torch into the trees every few seconds, lighting the way.

'Here, warm yourselves up,' he whispered, passing the boys a blanket each. Then he saw the tin. 'Is that the gun?'

Hal nodded and handed it over. He watched carefully as Kent took the bundle of fabric out, and he waited for the congratulations and thanks which were sure to follow. With the gun, they could arrest the bank robbers, tie them up and take their ship to the spaceport. Maybe even claim a big reward!

Instead, Kent took one look at the gun and shook his head. 'Sorry Hal. I'm afraid it's no good.'

'Is it broken?'

'No, it looks fine. Problem is, it's a flare pistol.'

Hal and Stinky exchanged a glance, but for once Stinky didn't have an answer.

'It's for emergencies,' explained Kent. 'When you're in trouble, you fire it into the sky. That way people know where you are.'

'I see,' said Stinky. 'And we're so far from anywhere, nobody would see the flare.'

'Exactly.'

Hal felt cheated. 'But if you point it at Ted and Amber . . . '

'They'll just laugh at us,' said Kent. 'It's dangerous enough, but it's not deadly.'

'But we walked all night to fetch it!' grumbled Hal.

'Oh, I'm sure it'll be useful. Just not the way we thought.'

'So what are we going to do?'

Kent thought for a moment. 'First, we have to get away from here. We'll take as much food and gear as we can carry, and follow the river down to the sea. It's going to be a long walk, and I'm afraid we'll have to live rough.'

‘We don’t need to walk,’ said Hal. ‘We can use the boat. It’s got a leak, but there’s a tin to bail it out.’

‘Excellent. That’ll make a big difference. Now, can you and Stinky grab some more food? I’ll make up a few bundles with the blankets.’

Hal crawled under the ship to the supplies, and he passed items back to Stinky one by one. Ted and Amber were sleeping just a few metres away, and every time a tin scraped or clinked he held his breath, worried the noise might wake them up. Worse, he couldn’t use a light to identify the tins, and for all he knew he was grabbing pickled cabbage, lumpy custard and washing powder.

After a few minutes collecting supplies, Hal felt Stinky tugging his ankle. He backed out and saw Kent Spearman separating tins into three piles: two small and one large. He tested the weight now and then, and when he was happy he bundled up the blankets and tied the tops together. ‘At least we won’t have to carry water,’ he said. ‘The river will supply all we need.’

Even so, the bundle of tins was heavy across Hal’s shoulder, and he was glad they wouldn’t be walking to the coast.

Spearman tucked the flare pistol into his belt. ‘All set?’

Hal and Stinky nodded.

'Okay. To the boat!'

◆

The sky was lighter by the time they reached the river, and Hal realised the sun would soon be up. He was tired and cold after the long night, and he was looking forward to a bit of warmth.

Kent was limping badly, even though his ankle was heavily strapped. He'd carried the heavy bundle of food all the way from the flyer, using a stout branch as a crutch, and he looked relieved to see the boat. After the disappointment with the gun, he'd probably been expecting a pair of wooden planks or a waterlogged raft. 'That'll do the job,' he said, nodding in approval. 'Put your stuff on the seats and we'll get her onto the water.'

They loaded the boat quickly, and Hal volunteered to push off. Before he did so, Stinky showed Kent the two branches, and he watched closely as the pilot lashed them together with good strong rope.

Then they were ready. They moved the boat to the shallows, Kent and Stinky climbed in, and as soon as they were settled Hal gave the wooden boat a shove and vaulted over the side.

They sailed into the middle of the river, where the current took hold of the boat. Kent used the branch like a tiller, straightening their course, and before long they were slipping past the silent trees. After a few minutes he passed the tiller to Hal, and picked up the bow. He unstrung it, then dug in the salvaged equipment for the tin of hooks.

'Are you going to fish?' asked Hal.

'We're all going to fish. We'll trail lines out the back, and maybe catch ourselves a nice breakfast.'

Hal's mouth watered. They'd had frozen fish cutlets on the Space Station once, with lots of tasty white flakes that had melted in his mouth. Imagine how much better fresh fish would be, especially when it was cooked over a fire!

Kent prepared several lines as well as the rod,

and he selected a tin of ham for the bait. They all dangled lines over the side, and nothing happened for several minutes. Then . . .

'It's pulling!' shouted Stinky. 'I've got one, I've got one!' He yanked on the line, and a big tangle of green weed landed in the boat.

Hal laughed at his friend's expression. 'Yum. Seaweed fritters. My favourite.'

'Try to keep the hook off the bottom,' said Kent.

Hal was still smiling to himself when his line went taut. At first he thought it was another weed, until the line shot sideways towards the bank. He pulled with all his might, and a mottled green fish landed in the bottom of the boat. It leapt and twisted, tangling the line, until Kent despatched it with a blow.

'Sorry, fish,' he muttered under his breath. 'Not your lucky day.'

Hal eyed the fish with mixed emotions. A minute ago it had been swimming around happily, and now it was breakfast. Still, they had to eat, and the fish hadn't suffered.

Ten minutes later there were half a dozen fish in the boat. Three were Hal's, Stinky caught two and Kent only caught one . . . the smallest of the lot. 'That'll do for now,' he said. 'We can't save the leftovers, so we'll just take what we can eat.'

'Are we going to cook them?'

'In a minute. Let me know if you see a dead tree.'

It was more like thirty minutes, but eventually Hal spotted a fallen tree in the woods. The branches were bare, white with age, and after a quick inspection Kent poled the boat towards the shore. They landed on a patch of sand, tied the boat up, and began snapping branches off the tree to make a fire.

Once it was alight Kent took the fish back to the river for cleaning, a process Hal wasn't too keen to watch. When the pilot came back the fish were skewered on branches. He gave the boys two each, and once the fire died down a little he showed them how to hold the skewers over the coals. The fish started to sizzle, and they turned them over and over until they were browned on both sides. When they were ready, Kent tried a mouthful. 'Its good. Just watch out for bones. Make sure you chew every mouthful.'

Hal tried his fish, and he gasped at the amazing flavour. Compared to this, the processed fish aboard the Space Station tasted like stale cardboard! Stinky was silent too, savouring every mouthful as though he'd never tasted anything better.

When they were finished Kent dug a hole, and

they buried the fish bones and scraped the remains of the fire in on top. Then he buried the ashes in dirt, stamping it down hard. 'That's how you leave a camping spot,' he said to the boys. 'As if nobody had ever been there.'

They returned to the boat, happy and full, and were just about to set off when Hal heard a rumble of thunder. 'Is that rain coming?'

'That's not thunder,' said Kent, staring up at the sky. 'It's a ship!'

— 25 —

Rapid escape

'You mean rescuers?' said Hal in excitement. 'Have they found us?'

'It seems like it,' said Kent thoughtfully. 'Unless . . .'

The thunder grew louder, and Hal saw a flash above the trees. He was about to wave both arms at it when Kent grabbed his wrist and hauled him under cover. 'Wh-what is it? What's the matter?'

'It's your friends, Ted and what's her name.'

'Amber?'

Kent nodded. 'I recognise the flyer.'

'It can't be,' said Stinky. 'They said the batteries were flat. They said –'

Hal snorted. 'They said they were hunters, Stinky. It was all lies.'

'They must be looking for us.' Kent gestured at

the boat. 'When they see that, they'll work out where we are soon enough.'

Roar! The flyer shot overhead, and Hal spotted a face in the sleek cockpit. It was Amber, and she seemed to be looking right at him. The flyer roared past and banked sharply, the ground shaking from the raw power of its engines.

'Why don't they land?' shouted Hal.

'Nowhere suitable,' said Kent. 'The bank isn't wide enough and they can't set down in the water.'

The flyer roared away, and everything was quiet again. 'Have they gone?'

'They'll land nearby and walk the rest. Come on, back to the boat.'

They hurried down to the water and pushed off. Once they were moving, Hal piped up again. 'I don't understand. What do they want us for?'

'They're hiding out in the woods, right? When we make it out of here we're going to report them, and the Peace Force will shut the whole area down. They'll never get away.'

'But they could fly away now. They have a whole planet to hide in.'

Kent shook his head. 'Every ship has a unique ID. If they fly anywhere else they'll be picked up by ground control.'

'So they're stuck in the woods?'

‘Yep. Trapped.’

‘But surely a proper search . . . ’

‘Hal, there are escape pods scattered all over Gyris, and this planet only has one rescue ship. The authorities will be looking for your classmates first, and until they’re safe they can’t turn their attention to Ted and Amber.’

‘Maybe we could shoot the flyer down?’

‘I admire your spirit, but our best bet is to evade them. We have the boat, so they’ll never catch us on foot. All they can do is fly around until we fetch up somewhere with a landing spot.’

‘Wh-what will they do to us?’ asked Stinky.

‘Nothing,’ said Kent. ‘They want to lie low until the fuss dies down, and they won’t want us giving away their position.’

‘We could promise not to tell.’

‘I don’t think they’d believe us, Hal.’

They floated down the river in silence, with Hal keeping one eye on the bank and another on the sky. Being hunted wasn’t pleasant, and for all he knew Ted and Amber might be armed. Then he tilted his head. Was that more thunder? It was very faint, but getting louder all the time. ‘They’re coming back!’ he shouted. ‘Quick, to the bank!’

Kent stood up, making the boat wobble, and dug the pole into the river. He gave a huge push, sending the boat towards the bank, then dragged the pole from the water for an even bigger heave.

Snap!

The pole broke in two, leaving half sticking out of the water with their shoelaces still attached. Hal could only watch helplessly as the boat continued on its way. Meanwhile, the roaring got louder. He searched the sky for the flyer, but the noise seemed to be coming from further down the river, as if Ted had landed and was waiting for them round the next bend.

Hal glanced towards the bank. The boat was travelling faster now, and the trees were moving past at quite a speed. It was too far to jump or swim, and their only option was to stay with the boat. The roar got louder and louder, and then they rounded the corner. Hal stared. It wasn't the flyer waiting for them, it was a narrow canyon filled with boulders. And the nice, gentle river wasn't flowing between the banks, it was smashing over the rocks with violent waves and vicious white water.

‘Rapids!’ shouted Kent in alarm. ‘Hold on for your lives!’

The next ten minutes were the most frightening of Hal’s life. Worse than getting stranded in space without any air, worse than the time he’d set fire to the Space Station’s canteen . . . it was even worse than the time his mum discovered he hadn’t washed his face for two weeks.

The boat leapt forward like a startled deer, plunging into the rapids before anyone was ready. Water came over the sides in waves, and the boat cannoned into one rock after another, shaking from end to end and nearly tipping over more than once. The noise was unbelievable, with shouting and roaring and the crashing of timber, and it was all Hal could do to hang on. Half their equipment flew out, vanishing without trace into the churning water, and the rest was hurled around the boat. Hal caught a tin can with his shin, which made him gasp in pain, and he saw Stinky clutching his elbow. His friend looked stunned and frightened, and Hal tried to give him a reassuring grin. Unfortunately his face was frozen in a fearsome grimace, which only made things worse.

Then . . . silence. They cleared the rapids, with the boat turning slow, soggy circles as it floated down the middle of the river.

'Is everyone okay?' asked Kent.

Stinky nodded, while Hal managed a brief 'yep'.

Kent found the bailer and set to work, throwing waves of water over the side. Hal gathered the remaining tins and stretched the blankets out to dry. It was mid-morning, and he wondered whether they'd still be damp by nightfall. Then he remembered the fishing gear, and he looked around the boat in growing despair. They'd lost the lot! And the gun? What about that? He couldn't see it at first, then spotted the tin jammed under Kent's seat.

'We had a lucky escape,' said Kent. 'If you hear a noise like that again, let me know straight away.'

'How will we get to the bank? The pole broke.'

'We'll paddle with our hands. Try it now.'

The river widened, and Hal saw a big sandbank to the right. He leant over the side and paddled for all he was worth, and with the other two assisting they moved the boat slowly to the edge of the river. They were just staggering out of the boat when he heard a low growl. 'Not wild animals too!' he muttered.

But no, it wasn't wild animals. It was the flyer.

— 26 —

Caught

Hal glanced at Kent, waiting for the next step in the escape plan, but the pilot shook his head. 'Sorry lads. It's time to call it quits. We barely have any food, and there could be more rapids around the corner.'

Hal pressed his lips together. How could they give up without a fight? Then he glanced at Stinky, and he realised Mr Spearman was right. They'd done their best, but his friend was out on his feet.

The flyer settled on the sandbank, blowing clouds of sand with its jets. Hal shielded his eyes from the grit, scowling as he saw Ted and Amber climbing out of the cockpit. They didn't seem to be armed, but the two of them could take Mr Spearman easily enough, and Hal and Stinky were no match for a pair of adults.

'There you are!' said Ted. 'We were worried about

you.'

'Give it up,' said Kent. 'We know who you are.'

Ted and Amber exchanged a glance. 'Fair enough,' said Ted at last. 'You're the pilot, right?'

'Kent Spearman.'

'Good. We need you to fly us out of here.'

Whatever Hal was expecting, that wasn't it.

'I'm sorry?' said Kent.

Ted jerked his thumb at the flyer. 'You're going to fly that to the next planet, with us onboard.'

Kent looked from one to the other. 'Why do you need me? Fly the thing yourself.'

'Neither of us is qualified for space flight.'

'It's easy. Just point the flyer straight up and hit the boost.'

'Neither of us knows the first thing about navigation.' Ted glanced at the sky. 'We don't want to get lost in space, do we?'

'That's a two seater,' said Kent, nodding towards the flyer. 'With you two and me . . . '

'It'll take three at a stretch.'

'What about the boys?' demanded Kent. 'You can't leave them out here on their own.'

'We'll leave them food and blankets, and when we're free and clear we'll notify the authorities.'

'That could be a day or two.'

'They'll survive,' said Amber shortly. 'It's either that or . . .'

'Okay, okay,' said Kent. 'I'll do it.'

Ted gestured towards the flyer. 'After you.'

'Wait. Let me talk to the boys first.'

'You've got five minutes.'

Kent turned to Hal. 'Sorry about this, but it's the only way. Now, do you remember how to make a fire?' Despite Hal's nod, Kent explained every step again, getting Hal to repeat them one by one. Once he'd got it, Kent explained how to build shelters and make their food last. Ted and Amber listened at first, but eventually started talking between themselves.

'I've got all that,' said Hal. 'But what about you? Will you be all right?'

'Don't worry, they'll let me go.'

'I don't trust them,' whispered Hal.

'Frankly, neither do I.' Kent glanced at Ted and Amber, who were arguing about something. Amber was gesturing with her finger, making a point, and Ted had both hands up. 'She's the danger. I don't think she likes loose ends.'

Then, before Hal knew what was happening, Kent pushed the flare pistol into his hands. It was heavy and warm to the touch.

'Hide it quickly,' murmured Kent. 'Behind your back.'

Hal did as he was told.

'Now, look at the flyer. Do you see the intake just behind the wing?'

Hal nodded.

'I'm going to lift off and hover above the ground, and then I'll turn the ship away from you. When I do, run up to it, aim the flare pistol at the intake and pull the trigger. Get close, one shot and run for it.'

Now that was more like it! Hal's heart thudded in his chest. 'What if the ship explodes? You might get hurt!'

'It won't, but the distraction will be very handy.'

'Come on, your time's up!' shouted Ted.

'Remember the plan,' murmured Kent. 'And keep that thing out of sight, or the game will be up.'

— 27 —

Flare

Hal watched Kent Spearman working the flyer's controls. When the pilot was ready he closed the cockpit and fired up the engines, blasting the boys with clouds of dust and grit. Hal squinted through the murk, trying to spot the signal. There! The lights flashed three times, and the ship rose into the air. It stopped about two metres up, and slowly turned away. Hal ran into the dust cloud, clutching the gun and struggling to breathe. The noise was intense, the engines hammering his ears.

The blast increased, and the flyer started to move. Desperately, Hal raised the gun and pulled the trigger.

Blam!

The gun bucked, and a bright spark bounced off the flyer and vanished into the trees. Hal frowned and aimed again.

Blam! Blam!

Two more shots, both wide of the mark. The first buried itself in the river, while the second almost parted Stinky's hair. Hal took the gun in both hands and sighted carefully, watching the wavering, dancing air intake through one eye. He didn't know how many shots the gun had left, and this one had to count.

Blam!

The shot streaked towards the flyer, and for a split second Hal thought he'd done it. The bright spark was heading for the air intake, just as Kent wanted. Then, at the last second . . . disaster! The flyer turned suddenly, and instead of hitting the intake, the flare went straight into the engine.

For a second, nothing happened. Hal lowered the gun, and the flyer's engines roared as it began to gain height. Surely they wouldn't get away?

Then . . . *crump!* The nearest engine exploded, bits of metal blasting from the exhaust. The flyer wobbled in mid-air, a loose engine cover flapping like a sheet of cardboard, and Hal and Stinky dived for the ground as the ship sailed overhead, trailing black smoke.

Hal uncovered his eyes just as the flyer splashed down, right in the middle of the river. There was a hiss as the cold water met the searing hot engines, and steam billowed up in waves, completely hiding the ship from view.

'Wow,' breathed Stinky. 'You've really done it this time.'

'He *told* me to do it!' protested Hal.

All was quiet, except for the cracking, bubbling noises from the ruined flyer. When the steam cleared Hal saw the ship sinking, with Kent struggling to get the cockpit open from the inside. Water was already lapping around the edge, and any second now the flyer was going to disappear for good.

The boys raced for the boat, pushing it out on the water and paddling like crazy, hurling spray far and wide as they crossed the river. Hal saw Kent waving him away, but he ignored the gestures. As soon as the boat bumped against the flyer he leapt up with a tin can in both hands, smashing it on the canopy with all his might. The toughened plastic didn't yield, and he saw Kent pointing at something. Under the cockpit there was a red and yellow handle, and Hal twisted and pulled until it came free.

Whoosh! The canopy rose into the air, and Kent immediately ducked out of view. Hal peered over the edge and saw Ted and Amber crammed into the rear seat, still struggling to undo their seatbelt.

Kent gave them a hand with the catch, then hauled them out one by one, helping them into the boat.

The flyer continued to settle, and water started pouring over the edge of the cockpit. 'Get clear!' shouted Kent.

'What about you?'

'I'm going to activate the emergency beacon. Go!'

Hal and Stinky paddled for shore, ignoring the stunned adults lying in the bottom of the boat. Behind them, the flyer started to list, electronics sparking and flashing inside the cockpit. Hal saw Kent Spearman with a microphone to his mouth, and then, without warning, the flyer slipped beneath the surface. Apart from an oil slick, there was nothing to show where it had been.

Hal stopped paddling and held his breath. Mr Spearman would emerge any second now, for sure. He had to!

— 28 —

The Deep

Seconds passed, and the water remained flat and still. Hal glanced at Stinky, who was frozen with shock. In the bottom of the boat, Ted and Amber looked as though the sky had just fallen on their heads.

Hal felt totally helpless. He didn't know how to swim, and he didn't have anything to reach underwater and hook Mr Spearman out of the cockpit. And even worse - Hal was the one who'd shot the flyer down. Nobody was going to believe Mr Spearman told him to!

There was a roar in the distance, and Hal stared at the sky. Was that thunder or another flyer?

Splaaassh!

At that second Kent Spearman broke the surface, his long hair plastered to his skull. He took a huge shuddering breath, shook the water from his eyes, then looked around for the boat.

'Over here!' shouted Hal.

Kent swam towards the boat with powerful strokes, and when he reached it he hooked one arm over the edge and guided it to the shore by kicking his legs. They were halfway there when Hal heard the low rumble again, and he scanned the sky. There was a dark spot in the distance, and as he watched it glinted in the sunlight. It *was* another flyer - maybe even rescuers looking for them!

They reached the shore, and Hal jumped out of the boat. 'I thought you'd drowned,' he told Kent. 'You were gone for ages!'

'I was trying to send a signal before the water killed the radio.'

'Did you do it?'

Kent shook his head.

'So what about that?' demanded Hal, pointing at the flyer. It was a long way away, and it seemed to be flying back and forth over a patch of sky.

'We need smoke, and lots of it. Time to light a fire.'

They'd completely forgotten about Ted and Amber, but Stinky's warning shout soon reminded them. Hal spun round and saw Stinky struggling in Amber's grip. 'Hey, let him go!'

'Nobody's going to get hurt,' said Ted. 'It's just a little insurance.'

'Help! Murder! Kidnap!' shouted Stinky, struggling for all he was worth.

'All right, take it easy,' said Kent. 'Everyone calm down.'

'You,' shouted Amber. 'Get that boat under the trees. Now!'

Hal realised what they were doing. If they hid the boat and got everyone under cover, the rescuers wouldn't see them from the air. Then he remembered the flare pistol, which was still tucked into his waistband. He reached behind his back and grabbed it, then pointed it directly at Amber. 'Hands up. Let Stinky go!'

Amber started to obey, then laughed. 'That's just a flare pistol! What are you going to do, light me?'

'Not quite.' Hal raised his hand above his head and pulled the trigger. There was a *whump!* as the gun fired, and a *whoosh!* as the flare shot into the sky. It sailed higher and higher, a tiny spark against the bright blue, and then . . . *Fizzz!* It burst into a dazzling white light.

The distant flyer continued on the same course for a few seconds, and then they heard it: a deep roar as it banked sharply and accelerated towards them. Amber and Ted took one look and bolted for the woods.

'Stop!' shouted Hal. 'Hands up!' The adults disappeared into the trees, and Hal was about to race into the forest waving the flare pistol.

Instead, Kent grabbed his arm. 'Let them be. The Peace Force will track them down in no time.'

'They couldn't find them before.'

'No, but they had a whole planet to search. Now they just have to cordon off this part of the woods. Trust me, those two will never get away.'

Hal felt cheated. He wanted to see the crooks marched away in handcuffs.

— 29 —

Camping

It was several days later, and Hal was sitting on a red plastic chair in front of a bright blue tent. There was a picnic table in front of him, with plastic knives and forks, paper serviettes and a tablecloth decorated with trees and plants. Hal was toying with a plate of food, with vegetables and cheese and cubes of meat all cut into neat shapes, and he wasn't happy.

'This isn't real camping,' he muttered under his breath. 'This is a picnic in the playground!'

Stinky rolled his eyes. They'd joined their classmates at the campsite after the rescue, and Hal had done nothing but complain ever since. 'The beds are too soft, the water's too clean, the grass is all smooth and even . . . is there anything you like about this place?'

'No,' said Hal shortly.

‘So you’d rather be lost in the woods with a pair of criminals?’ Stinky waved his arms. ‘You’d prefer that to swimming, and games, and campfires, and sing-alongs?’

Hal groaned.

‘And eggs and bacon for breakfast, and steak for dinner, and –’

‘The food out of those old cans tasted better than this.’

Stinky was about to protest, but then he nodded. ‘I suppose eggs and bacon does get boring after a while.’

‘And they ring bells for lunch, and dinner,’ muttered Hal. ‘And they won’t let us fish, or hunt, or build a real shelter.’

Stinky nodded. The bows had been confiscated within minutes, and hadn’t been seen since. Hal’s attempts to make more had failed dismally, and he’d been banned from cutting any more branches, or ’borrowing’ twine.

‘I wish they’d never rescued us,’ said Hal.

‘Never mind. We’re going home tomorrow.’

‘Is that supposed to make me feel better? My new tutor is making up so many lesson plans I’ll still be studying when I’m fifty.’ There was a commotion near the gift shop, and Hal’s voice tailed off as he watched a dark blue car pulling up. It had Peace

Force badges on the side, and a dozen lights and sirens on the roof. Two officers stepped out, one of them a short, overweight man, and the other a tall, slender woman. The short man went into the shop, and a few seconds later there was an announcement over the PA system.

Would all children please come to the barn for an important event. I repeat –

'Quick, let's sneak away,' said Hal.

Stinky displayed the orange band on his wrist. 'We're all tagged, remember?'

Hal remembered all right. The campsite was surrounded by a safety fence, and crossing it triggered an alarm. He'd set it off half a dozen times on his first day, until they threatened to feed him nothing but spinach for the week.

'Come on,' said Stinky. 'It might be something interesting.'

Hal snorted, but he followed his friend to the barn. It was a large building, with mock timber walls that were actually made from sheets of plastic. There were rows of seats for the audience, and Hal and Stinky sat at the back. The two Peace Force officers glanced at their watches, then took to the stage.

'Good afternoon,' said the female officer. 'Tell me, are Hal Junior and Steven Binn here?'

Everyone looked at Hal and Stinky.

'Would you come up the front please?'

Hal groaned. Now what? Was it the home-made porridge he'd cooked over the campfire, or the boat he'd tried to make out of picnic tables, or his repeated attempts to remove the hated orange band from his wrist? Whatever it was, it had to be bad. They didn't send two Peace Force officers for nothing.

Hal and Stinky made their way to the front, ignoring the whispers from the crowd. When they got there, the officers smiled, and the female one took up the microphone again. 'As you know, these two boys had quite an adventure, and thanks to their initiative and bravery two dangerous criminals are behind bars.'

Hal was shocked. They weren't there to punish him, they were saying thanks!

'As a reward, we'd like to present you with these Peace Force cadet medals.' The officer nodded to her partner, who gave each of the boys a polished wooden box. Hal peeked in his, and his eyes widened as he saw the official-looking badge. How cool was that!

'There's also a small gift for each of you, by way of thanks.'

The sweating officer returned with two brand-new rucksacks in Peace Force blue, setting them on the floor. Hal opened his, and his eyes lit up when he saw the compact tent, the super-light sleeping bag, the neat little cooking stove and the clever stack of pots, pans and plates. Then his face fell. They were going back to the Space Station the next day. What was he going to do with camping equipment?

The officer glanced at her watch, then continued. 'There was supposed to be another guest, but –' She stopped. A groundcar had just drawn up nearby, and there was a thud as the door closed. They heard pounding footsteps, and everyone turned to the door just as Kent Spearman hurried in. Instead of wearing his pilot outfit, he was decked out in jeans and a padded jacket, and he was wearing big black hiking boots.

'Sorry I'm late! I got a speeding ticket.'

'I'm sure we can sort that out for you,' said the officer drily. 'Now, would you like to say a few words?'

'Sure thing. Thanks to these two I've been offered a great new job. I just wanted to say thanks in public, and give them a gift of my own.' Kent reached into his pocket and took out a matching pair of utility knives, with blades, scissors, pliers and even a little magnifying glass. He gave one each to Hal and Stinky, and Hal resolved to try the sharpest blade on his orange bracelet the minute he was alone.

The officer wrapped up the ceremony, and after the applause died down, Hal drifted outside with the rest.

'So, how are you both?' asked Kent.

Hal shrugged.

'Enjoying the camping?'

Hal pulled a face.

'That good, huh? Here, take a look at this.' Kent led them to his car and opened the trunk. Inside was a big rucksack, stuffed with camping gear. There was also a bundle of fishing rods. 'I start my new job in a week, but before that I'm going to explore these woods properly. Fishing, camping, sleeping under the stars . . . it's going to be great.'

Hal sighed. 'It sounds fantastic.'

'So, I got to wondering. How'd you two like to come along? I never did show you how to hunt properly.'

A whole week of real camping! Hal's eyes shone. 'That would be amazing!'

'Fantastic!' added Stinky.

'Do we get bows and arrows?' asked Hal quickly.

'Of course!' said Kent. 'And fishing rods, too.'

Then Hal remembered something, and his spirits crashed. 'It's no good. We're going home tomorrow. We can't miss our flight or we'll get in trouble.'

Kent laughed. 'I'm a space pilot, remember? When the week's up I'll fly you home myself.'

'Yes, but . . . ' Hal sighed. 'My new tutor's got lessons ready for me, and mum won't let me miss school, and –'

'Don't worry, I've already cleared it with your folks. Your dad says the Space Station will survive without you for a few more days. In fact, your dad says they're enjoying the peace and quiet.'

— 30 —

Real camping

The next week was the most exciting - and exhausting - of Hal and Stinky's lives. They hiked over hills, climbed mountains, and explored deep valleys with thundering waterfalls. They camped wherever they liked, they hunted their own food and learned to clean & cook it for themselves. They used their bows, the fishing rods, their special utility knives, and all their brand new camping equipment. Kent Spearman showed them how to navigate by the stars so they didn't get lost, and he taught them how to set a proper fire, build a shelter, and survive in the rough. The boys grew tanned under the sun, and fitter than they'd ever been aboard the Space Station.

When the glorious week finally ended, and they boarded the shuttle for the flight home, Hal Junior promised himself that one day he'd live in the wild, sharing with nature and getting away from civilisation.

In between piloting his own spaceship and saving the Galaxy from evil, of course!

Acknowledgements

With thanks to my loyal readers, Tricia and Ian.

If you enjoyed this book, please leave a brief review at your online bookseller of choice. Thanks!

About the Author

Simon Haynes was born in England and grew up in Spain. His family moved to Australia when he was 16.

In addition to novels, Simon writes computer software. In fact, he writes computer software to help him write novels faster, which leaves him more time to improve his writing software. And write novels faster. (www.spacejock.com/yWriter.html)

Simon's goal is to write fifteen novels before someone takes his keyboard away.

Update 2018: goal achieved and I still have my keyboard!

New goal: write thirty novels.

Simon's website is spacejock.com.au

The Hal Junior series ...

The *first* book in the Hal Junior series!

Don't forget ...

The *second* book in the Hal Junior series!

And …

The *third* book in the Hal Junior series!

And ...

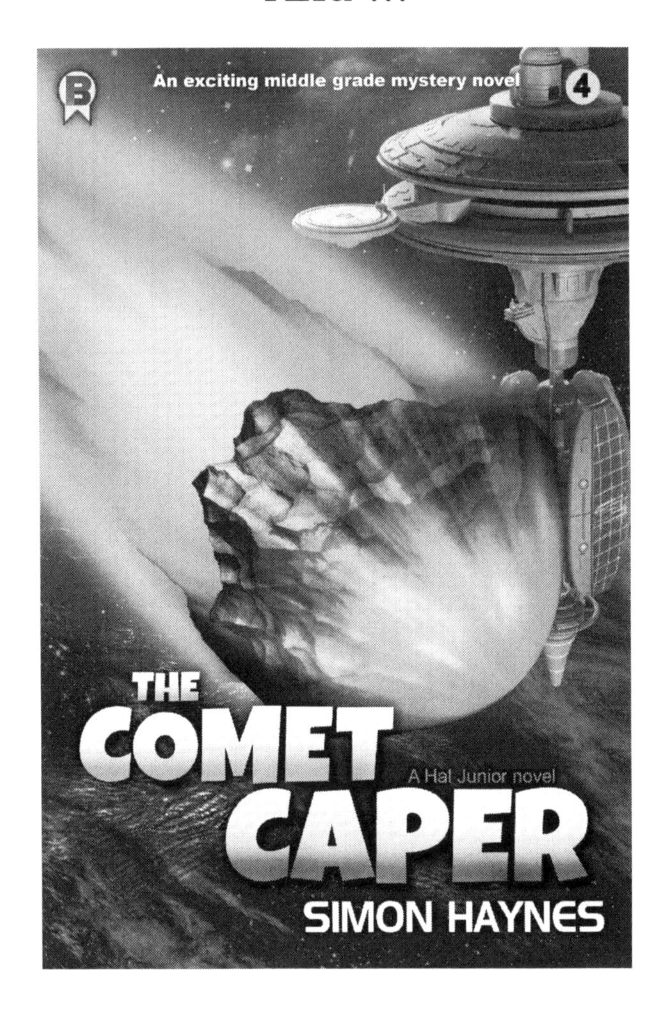

The *fourth* book in the Hal Junior series!

Printed in Great Britain
by Amazon

77430188R00123